# DIAMOND

Wendy Turner

# Author Works under Wendy Tarasoff or Pen Name, Wendy Turner

## Books found on Amazon.com

### *Children's Books*
Scare Away the Dark
Dragon's Pearl
Freddie, the Talking Mouse (English Version)
Freddie, the Talking Mouse (Spanish Version)

### *Adult Fiction – Pen Name*
Diamond, a Romance Murder Thriller (English Version)
Diamond, a Romance Murder Thriller (Spanish Version)

### *Non Fiction – Pen Name*
Secret Sauce of Sentences

*This is a work of fiction with fictional characters…*

**Turtle Publications**
203-150 Van Horne Street
Penticton, BC V2A 4K2
1-250-460-3258

Email: wtarasoff7@gmail.com

Website: https://turtle-publications.now.site/

ISBN: 978-0-9918581-8-7

# Acknowledgments

I would like to say thank-you to my family and to those that contributed to this story—Joy, Christine, Louise, Lindsay, Seann, Frank, and Dawn.

# DIAMOND

The bullet whizzed through the air, hitting the target; another bullet cut razor sharp into the surrounding air, and hit its mark. Matt Lando's arms dropped, and his hands fell to his sides. He knew full well he might have to take another life. He sighed; he took in the air, sucked it down deep inside and finally let it go. Matt Lando wanted to know if he could—if he would—do it again if he had to.

Pickett stood next door to him at the shooting range, and pointed to the outline of a person. He cocked his gun; a bullet went into the air, cutting it like an open wound. "Matt, it is always different with a body." The dummy target fell to the ground just like Matt's, touching the blades of grass…then unbearable silence.

"Nothing prepares you for the real thing, the howls of pain. Nothing, Pickett, nothing…." Out of the line of fire, Matt turned his attention to their highly trained police dogs that had seen combat. Both were sitting, waiting. Matt watched as Pickett lay down his gun, putting the safety on. The guns were secure. Together, they walked the dogs over to the K-9 training area. The dogs needed to run over the obstacle course, their ears on full alert.

Both men took a moment to discuss life.

"She must have red hair," dreamed Matt, brushing his brown beard with his hands. "I saw her last night, a real picture of her. I am going to try online dating."

"Get me one, too! She must be blonde," answered Pickett. Today he is wearing a blue t-shirt and denim. He pointed that out to Matt, "Seems we're on the same page denim and blues."

"Shooting off a gun as a profession sometimes scares women away, the right kind of woman."

"The right red headed woman would not scare easily."

"Same with the blonde, she must be smart."

They laughed together about it. After the dogs were finished on the course, the two men packed up their guns, got into their cars, and drove their separate ways. Each took their dog with them in the back seat.

Matt headed downtown, winding through a semi-desert highway next to Okanagan Lake into the heart of the Penticton. It was a lazy day in the haze of the early afternoon summer sun. Matt was thinking of the picture he saw of her…. He wondered if she was available to date. Who knows she might be the one. He would send her a message. Those blue eyes….

Red headed Sara was at home sitting in her den wearing a pair of pink rabbit-eared slippers, and denim jeans with a blue t-shirt. Today's project was to wrap up her digital marketing plan for the Zorteck Corporation out of Vancouver. She printed the plan out to make editing corrections, and put a sticky note on it—FB ads? Google ads? Costs?

She only worked in the mornings, so her afternoon was free to shop. She had plans to pick up a dress. She might take Jen, best friend, with her if she was free, but her two-year-old son was a handful (Jen chased him everywhere).

Sara loved her own business created by cobbling different jobs together for online marketing and books. She put her pen down, noting the time was noon–time to eat. Then, go out for that dress. She called Jen on the baby monitor.

"Jen?"

"What?"

"Up for some shopping?"

"Just got back, sorry."

"Okay, touch base, later."

Sara snacked on a piece of ham and a salad. She went to her computer to look up her messages. There was one from a Matt Lando. She liked the name. His profile offered some insight–tall, two inches above her height, brown hair with a beard. Seems he's asking for a date.

She grabbed her keys and purse and headed out the door.

To Matt, she's a mystery—both light and dark. Some light bounces back, but only a portion of it from the picture. He sees her light in angles but that is just the surface. She's full of complicated prisms, he knows that. He absorbed her picture on Plenty of Fish, and wondered whether life with her would be a rainbow effect, or whether she would swallow him whole.

He studied her features—red hair, shoulder length, and her smile that radiated. Her blue eyes shone. If she lived in the same city, it would make it possible to meet her, maybe, on the street. Sure enough, she did.

He never expected to meet her by accident in a pair of red shoes and a summery dress. But there she was in heels walking so close to him when her heel broke. He caught her in mid-flight next to his car.

"I've got you," he said, smelling her gentle vanilla fragrance. He lifted her to her feet, opened his car door, and sat her down gently on the seat.

She smiled in red lipstick. "Thank you."

"Did you sprain your ankle?"

"Yes, a bit."

"May I?" He felt her ankle. "Just bruised. Suggest staying off that for a few days. My name is Matt, Matt Lando."

"Are you in the habit of rescuing women, Matt?" She chuckled. "Sara Diamond."

"I think we need to get that shoe off."

"Sure."

"Interesting, 3 inch heel, size 8."

"What!? Do you have a shoe fetish?"

Matt held the shoe up, and said, "It is a dance shoe! Stiletto heel. Can you tell me where you bought it?"

"I checked all over the city, and I found it at Shoe Haven, three blocks from here on 5th."

"I just need to know where I can buy another pair for you. Do you live near here?"

"Yes, within walking distance."

"I'll drive you home then?" he smiled.

She nodded. He seems nice for a Matt, and she settled into the passenger seat. He was strong and had a good vibe. He drove carefully, deliberately.

"To the right, second house."

He parked the car, and came around and lifted her right out of the car, and placed her down on the doorstep.

"May I keep this shoe? Dinner at 7. I'll bring the shoes." He grinned, and ran away with the shoe, and he yelled from a distance, "Don't worry, I'll carry you, if necessary." Then he was gone.

Sara thought *he's so cute—funny about the shoes. I'll bring some extra money to pay for them. My favorite ones too! Seems odd he's so focused on them.* "Oh well, maybe he was a shoe salesman in another life." Sara took out her keys, unlocked the door, and hobbled into the house.

***

Matt Lando came into his office at 4:30 pm dropping a plastic bag marked Shoe Haven on his second chair. On his desk at police headquarters were three new case files—murder, jewelry robbery, and purse snatcher. Standard day! His job as a detective was to look for that one slim fact.

Partner Nicky Pickett came over with two cups of coffee. "Looking at the crime photos?"

Matt looked at three different photos. One was a beautiful woman, possibly mid-30's shot and found murdered in her house; one was of an elderly lady; the last one was a jewelry store with diamond necklaces under violently smashed glass.

"Any commonalities?" said Pickett, "Before we ship them to different officers?"

Staring at the photos, Matt studied the details. Then it struck him as odd that there was only one shoe in each photo. "Pickett, look at the shoe."

"What?"

"The one red shoe on the right of the body!" Matt grabbed the bag marked Shoe Haven, and pulled out the shoes from the shoe box. "Look, it is the same ones! Stiletto heel."

"Yes, but Matt everyone wears shoes. The woman was strangled and shot."

Matt took out a magnifying glass, and looked closely at the shoe in the woman's photo. "I think there is more to it. See?" Matt handed the magnifier to Picket. "Look at what is on the shoe."

Pickett focused the magnifier, "Looks like glass...."

"Or a diamond."

"Let's have the photos blown up bigger to make sure."

Matt grabs the rest of the file and rifles through it. He finds the evidence log, "Pickett? The log shows one diamond."

"Crap. The cases may be connected. Matt, why do you have the same pair of red Stiletto shoes…?"

\*\*\*

Matt arrived at Sara's house at 7 pm. Timing is everything; he grinned and knocked at the door. And there she was in a beautiful blue dress. She looked at him with those eyes.

"You are here," she smiled. "Come in."

He looked into the room and noted the chocolate couch.

"Sit."

"Here are your shoes."

Sara opened the shoe box, and then left Matt for her bedroom, and put the shoes in the closet.

"Thank you, Matt. Do you always buy a woman shoes on the first date?"

"No, I never have. This is a first."

She came out of the bedroom with a pair of slippers on, and some money from her purse. "How much, Matt?"

"Oh no, these were paid for along with the dinner," turning her down firmly. How's your foot?"

"Still sore.

 "Give me your arm and we will go."

"Jen?"

"Who?"

"Jen Weber, my girlfriend. She lives next door." Sara pointed to the kitchen counter, "Baby monitor for her baby, Kevin. He's two, and I babysit."

Matt nods.

"Jen?"

"Yes."

"We are going now, Jen."

***

Jen Weber sat drinking coffee. On the table were two baby monitors, one for Kevin, and the other for Sara's place next door.

"Today's TV Crime Beat News at 7:30 pm for Saturday, 25th.

"31-year-old woman found dead in her home in the 100 block of Marpole area, Friday. Police investigating.

"Jewelry robbery on High Street at diamond store. Man seen fleeing with estimated 2 million.

"Purse snatcher seen running south on High Street left behind a diamond and a red shoe claims elderly woman. He took my purse too."

Jen was miffed. She turned off the TV remote. She didn't want to hear any more automatic voices.

One of the monitors started to speak. Usually Sara called out when she was home. "Hello?" No answer. Someone…Jen was on alert. He was looking at her through the window, peering into her kitchen. Then a dark voice spoke….

"I saw you on the street. Super sexy. I followed you home…. I have the red shoe. Love the smell of new leather. I will be back. Now, I will go and pay the old lady a visit. He unzipped what sounded like a purse. Yes, here's her address." Papers fell on the floor. Sara's flower vase that Jen had given her for her birthday last year fell broken. "I always get my diamonds back, my pretty."

Jen held her hand over her mouth. The male voice had his hands on the baby monitor at Sara's. There was heavy breathing into the monitor and the voice said, "I'll get you too."

There was a sudden noise, and the breaking of glass through Jen's kitchen window. She wasn't sure what it was and went to see–a bullet in the back door! It was lodged in just half way. She pried the bullet out and called out for her husband. "Carl? Carl! No, he's at work, at work!" She picked up her cell phone to dial. "He's in Sara's house. Carl, come home now! Maybe he's the murderer. He said he would murder me too, Carl."

"Lock yourself and the baby in the bathroom. Take your cell. I'll call the police. There was a diamond on a red shoe in the closet this morning. Did you lose it from your wedding ring?"

"No??!! A diamond? Did you say red shoe? I don't own a red shoe." Jen was frantic. She grabbed Kevin off the floor, ran up the stairs with the phone, and locked herself in. "Sara, Sara, don't go home!" Jen rang the number. "Come on, come on, Sara, pleaaase pick up."

\*\*\*

"This is a nice place, Matt." Sara took in the small tables with candles, and white table cloths with real rose petals, and Matt sat her down in a corner spot looking out onto Okanagan Lake. "What's the name of this hideaway?"

"The Beacon."

"Do you come here often?"

"Yes, when I wish to sit and read a book, or bring a serious date on a Saturday night."

"Whoa. Slow down and at least let me have some dinner."
She laughed.

Matt took her hand and looked into those blue eyes.
"Well, we'll order, shall we? Would you like the salmon
special?

"I'll have that, and a glass of red wine."

The waitress took her order.

"I'll have the same, and a mug of beer. I saw you on
Plenty of Fish, you know, so it seems we have fish in
common. How long have you been on the site, Sara?"

"Just a few days, actually."

"What's my competition like?"

"Mint."

"Mint?"

"Yes, I see the salmon is served with some springs of
mint. Nice touch."

"Your hands are so soft, Sara. You are very good at the
changing of a subject!"

"So you are serious then. What do you do for a living,
Matt?"

"I see you are very sexy with a fork. The salmon is to die
for, and the mint is my special touch at your command.
I own the Beacon, and I am a police homicide detective."

"Wow," she stopped for a moment, salmon on the fork.

He took her into the kitchen where he put on his white hat. "Come meet the chef…." He took her in his arms. "May I have this first kiss?"

It was about 7:45 pm when Sara got the call, and put it on speaker phone, but Jen was very upset and speaking too fast, and all she got out of it was "murderer…red shoe…diamond…in the house, don't–", and the line went dead. Sara tried to call her back, but no answer.

***

By 9 pm, Sara and Matt had met police at Jen's house. Jen and Carl and baby Kevin were all outside in the dark.

Jen was cold, shaking to the touch, and Carl grabbed little Kevin out of her arms. "Sara!" Jen called out. "He was in your house, mine too! Sara…I am so scared."

"What's going on, Matt?"

Matt said, "I will be right back, Sara." He moved toward the other officers. "What's happened, Pickett?"

"He was gone when we got there, but in Sara's house there were some papers on the floor. They belong to Edna King, remember the purse snatching case? We went to the address to check it out, but she was dead, strangled: We feel that it is unsafe for Sara and Jen to stay home at the present time."

"God, now we have two bodies in the morgue."

"Crap! Must be one mad son of a bitch! He tore Edna's place apart looking for something. It is my guess that he knows the names of his victims before he kills them."

Matt walked back to Sara and Jen with K-9 Perry, his dog.

"Can't tell you much about the investigation, but it is not safe for you here. We will pay for you to stay at a hotel."

"We?"

"The police, Jen. I am with the police. Matt Lando, Lead Homicide Detective."

"Homicide?" said Carl. "There has been a homicide?"

"Yes."

"Jen pulled Sara aside and whispered, "There's a bullet. Here, Sara. Put it in your pocket."

Sara did so without thinking.

***

Matt and Pickett were back in the office early the following morning to look at the paperwork on the cases, and to make a visit to the morgue at 10 am.

"Seems she was shot in the head, too," said Matt.

"Look at the Edna King photos. There is a diamond necklace with six missing diamonds."

"Wonder, what is the significance of the number? Are they already dead? Or are they about to be dead?"

"I think Sara and Jen are on that list."

"Me too. We also have to check out the video from the jewelry store, and maybe we will get lucky on some prints. Those should be in soon Pickett." Looking at his watch, Matt said, "Ten has almost arrived. Steve hates it when we are late."

They took the elevator to the basement.

Walking into the morgue, the smell of moth balls weighed heavily in the air, and in everything including the flooring had the smell of death. They hit a wall of it as soon as they opened up the doors where Steve waited.

"First to Edna King..." Steve proceeded lifting the sheet. "She was struck on the back of the head. She was strangled with what I suspect was the nearest thing that had a cord, perhaps a toaster as the cord was still around her neck– considerable bruising. Shot. Now, to the 31-year-old woman, she now has a name, Kate Taylor, single mother of two. Same type of bruising, likely from a telephone extension cord found next to the body. Shot in the head. You will have to notify next of kin. Here are all the full reports."

"What about prints?" said Matt.

"I have it here. There are no prints."

"How is that possible? He has been in three places perhaps four."

"The photo shows the prints have been melted off from his fingers, but maybe they will still identify him if we can match him directly to them. Crap. We have to catch this guy, and we still have to put it in the database. I don't hold out much hope for that," ranted Pickett.

"When Frank gets a hold of this, he's gonna have to release a statement to the media, and it's going to go serial," countered Matt.

***

It was a long day reviewing the evidence, and chasing down any kind of a lead, and what was needed now was a detailed accounting of Sara's life, especially her routines. He thought it best he interviewed her over dinner at the Beacon.

He had Plenty of Fish open on his laptop, and saw that Sara had responded back to his profile. He typed.... "When we met, and you broke your shoe, I fell in love with you. Because of the investigation, and because I can't wait to see you, where are you staying in the hotel? Dinner out?"

"Room 207."

Are you okay?

"Yes, we are managing. Don't know what will happen next. I can see Lake Okanagan. What a view."

"Be there in 10."

He whisked her away with 20 questions.... "I would like to know everywhere you have gone in the last few weeks. Next of kin? How often do you go to Shoe Haven? What's your favorite dish to eat? Are there any men in your life (besides me that is)?" He kissed her hand.

Sara was overwhelmed by the barrage. She insisted that they have dinner in peace. What was with men anyways, especially, the last question was not related to the case. He was just interested in whether he had any competition!

"Sara, there was a missing shoe in your closet and a diamond. Are they yours? One of your shoes is missing, and…"

"Wait, what?"

"Jen, had the same thing in her closet. Who do you know jointly?"

Sara's head was spinning. For sure, she was not eating the fish this time.

"My shoe is missing, and there is a diamond?"

"Yes, we think it is part of his signature. Sara, you are in danger so is Jen. I am leaving Perry with you at overnight, and I am staying the night as well. In the morning, I will get you a security dog." He gave her hand a squeeze. "I don't want to lose you. And I will assign another dog for Jen and her family. You both can't go home."

What Matt wanted to say, but couldn't, was that he and Pickett had the video footage from the jewelry store robbery and Shoe Haven. If he was in there maybe Shoe Haven was one of his favorite haunts. All Matt wanted to do is shelter Sara from a man that was ruthless. He paid cash. Next thing to do was to check video footage of local banks and ATM's. No woman was safe, and Matt knew he would strike again, and soon....

*\*\**

Matt spoke to Frank, Detective Sergeant, as he was preparing for a press conference. "We have to give women of the city a warning that this man is deadly."

"Yes, and we know what the press will call him then, 'The Diamond Strangler'". Frank walked up to the microphone outside police headquarters. "We have reason to believe there is a dangerous predator of women in the city. He sneaks into homes, and leaves a red shoe and a diamond, and then comes back later to strangle. Shoots them dead. Women, please report such items in your closet to the police immediately."

There was mumbling from the press gallery...shoe...gun...diamond...strangler.

"Questions...?"

"What are the police doing to protect women?"

"Our first duty is to get this out to the public. An investigation is underway. Phone lines will be open to the women of our city."

"Is there a description?"

"Male, approximately 5'7", dark hair."

"Where is he getting the red shoes?"

"If your red shoes, ladies, are also missing we would also like you to report."

"...?"

"...?"

"Diamond Strangler."

"It is all in the statement. Thank you."

For Matt these details could not get out to the public fast enough. Minutes mattered, and Matt and Pickett had six more banks to go to for footage, and 27 ATM's. *Sara, dearest, Sara. The dog is guarding. It will be okay, okay. I will check in with you later. Be safe my darling one.*

***

At 9 am the following morning, Sara was going through her pockets looking for her keys when she pulled out the bullet. She had forgotten all about it. Jen knocked at the door, and the security dog had his ears back when Sara answered.

Sitting down at the kitchen table in her room next to a laptop, Jen blurted out, "News was just on. They died a double death of a gunshot, and strangulation."

"Both?"

"Gosh, he wanted to make sure they were dead."

"Two? A serial killer?" Sara opened her hand and there was the bullet. "We are going to have to tell Matt."

"I know, but I have been watching CSI, and there is suppose to be a serial number on here somewhere. Let's have a closer look."

Sara passed the bullet to Jen, and went through her purse looking for her magnifying glass. "Every woman has one in there, right? Found it. Here Jen."

"Thank God for that. The print would be really tiny."

"Look, what does it matter? It's evidence."

"There is no serial number on it, Sara. Let's Google it."

"What do you mean? We know nothing."

"Exactly. Google 'untraceable gun'".

"Ghost gun?!!"

"Ghost bullets?"

"A Liberator was the first 3-D pistol. The USA has some States where ghost guns are legal. How do they then trace the gun to an owner?"

"They don't, Jen. Fingerprints?"

"Oh, no," Jen had her fingers on the bullet.

"Maybe he's trying to liberate his victims? What does a gun say about its owner? Maybe he has access to a 3-D printer?"

Jen and Sara sat there in silence. Both looked at the other and didn't drink a drop of coffee after it was poured.

Jen spoke first, warming both hands on her cup, "He's deadly."

"He plans things. What are we going to do?"

"Where would he get the bullets?"

"Google it."

"How to build a ghost gun?"

"Yep. Let's Utube that."

"My God, we can actually build one—video step by step instructions!"

***

Matt and Pickett are reviewing videos from the jewelry store, and Haven Shoes at the police station at 8:30 am on a Sunday.

"How much video tape did we ask for, Pickett?"

"Two weeks worth."

"Heavy slogging."

Put the jewelry tape in first. Witness descriptions say he's about 5'7", skinny, and wore a mask. There, he's there with a Glock 21."

The video shows him speaking to the clerk, pointing directions out with the gun. He doesn't go for the cash, but for the diamonds, smashing a few cases, and he takes the necklace they found at the Edna King crime scene. He pushes the clerk towards the back of the store, looking for the safe. "If anyone pushes the panic button, I will kill you."

"Let's go back two weeks and move forward, Pickett."

"I will set up the video for Haven Shoes. I want to see if he shows up there. Maybe, we'll get lucky."

"There. He's 5'7" and so is the guy in the background out the store window, and we can't rule out the clerk either."

"Okay, it's a start."

"Let's get that guy in the window blown up so we can see him and his dimples."

Pickett moves the tape forward. "Look, he's there again outside the window with a clear view of the till."

"He's stalking."

"Maybe. Move the tape forward. He's just peering in, watching things."

"Check out the staff at Shoe Haven for any boyfriends."

"Got it."

"Send the voice to the audio unit, and all the reports to the profiler."

***

Outside of Shoe Haven he stood, watching, waiting. He didn't care for the man that owned the store. "Yes, she's buying the right heels, the red ones on sale." *Red is my favorite color although I will take those ones later, but when he had asked the store manager earlier, he had only six pairs of red ones left, dumb ass. She has great legs, doesn't she? This one will be fun.*

He went into the store and stood behind her. The clerk asked for her phone number.

"250-555-0999. I know my friend, Jill, will like these too."

He now had her phone number.

He followed her, down the street to her car, putting on his mask. She opened her side passenger door; he moved past her, grabbing her purse on the seat and ran. He left the shoes. Time to savor those later....

***

When she got home, she called the police and reported the incident. She never mentioned the red shoes because they weren't stolen. She started to call the credit card companies, and then she called Jill and spoke on the phone for over two hours. She put on the new shoes and a red lace dress.

He was watching from his car. He called her number. "Jill asked me to call you for a date."

"Who are you?"

"My name is Jeff. Want to go out for a drink?"

"Sure, why not?"

"5 at the Edge Bar on 9th."

"See you there."

He looked her up on social media. He found all the personal information he would ever need. He studied it for the next few hours.

***

Matt and Pickett had a group meeting of officers to go over the day's cases that had not yet hit their desk and about the hot line. After the news, there were always a flash of calls to handle, and Matt asked his staff, "How many new cases?"

Various officers answered with the number.

Murders? None

Burglaries? Two

Purse snatchers? One.

"Tell me about the last one."

"Young woman, 30's, on 5th."

"Where on 5th?"

"Near the corner of 5th and Elm."

"What is near there?"

"A few restaurants and Shoe Haven."

"The address of the woman, and the phone number, now!"

Matt and Pickett were out the door and into the car *fast*.

Pickett was always after Matt about his bullet attitude with the staff, but Matt was listening this time.

"We should give them more information, and then they would know."

"Yes, but this was the first briefing, Pickett remember that."

"Pickett, what's the name? Get on the phone and call her."

"Hello, Melissa? This is the police...are you alone? Yes. I want you to take your phone and walk quickly, but quietly, over to the next door neighbor's place...and stay on this line. Do not make any noise even to close the door. Can you do that?"

"Yes.... What's this about?"

"Is it a house or apartment?"

"House."

"Can you do that right now, Melissa?"

Melissa looked out her living room window. There was a man in a car sitting there. "Is that you in the car?"

"No, there will be two of us."

"Melissa, you have a back door? Go out the back way. Maintain silence on the phone until you get inside again."

"...."

Matt was on the radio, "Get an unmarked car out here. There is a guy parked on the street in front of 345 Graves Street. Pull in behind the car without any lights or sirens on. Get a license plate and a clear photo if you can. Send two women, less suspicious. And sit on him, everywhere he goes, you go."

"Matt, he's gone. Will see about camera footage."

"Melissa? Melissa."

"Yes, I am here"

"Are you inside?"

***

Matt is on the phone to Sara. "I'm sorry. I haven't been in touch for a few days what with the murder investigation.

"I get it."

"I would like to make it up to you with dinner at the Beacon, and then, we can go for a walk on the pier? Pick you up you at 7:00?"

"Okay. See you then."

Matt and Pickett walked to the house behind 345 Graves and knocked on the door. Over a cup of tea, they had a chat with Melissa.

"So, can you go over, Melissa, what you did today?"

"It was just regular shopping."

"What stores did you go into and what did you purchase?"

"I went for coffee, and then I purchased some red dance shoes. I have them on now. Nice, eh? I have a date with Jeff."

"And who is Jeff? Is he new?"

"Yes, he called and said he knew Jill."

"Did Jill ever mention him before?"

"Come to think of it, no."

"Call Jill. Put her on speaker phone."

Melissa reached Jill and asked the question of whether she knew Jeff at all.

"No, I don't know a Jeff, Melissa."

Matt's phone and Pickett's rang. They moved outside to take the call. It was a conference call from the profiler.

"Your guy is older, and he likes to toy with his victims in private before he kills them. He's likely to follow them, and even ask them for a date to gain access to the house is my guess. No forced entry. Both victims had dinner shortly before they died. There is more, but I figured this was more immediate."

"Pickett, Jeff may be our guy."

"Melissa, when are you supposed to meet Jeff?"

"At 5:00 pm at the Edge Bar."

*** 

"Matt, there is no time for a witness statement, and it is already 3:00 pm. She meets him at the bar at 5?"

"She either meets him or we lose our chance."

"Right. He knows who she is. We can't put a plain clothes officer in there."

Matt and Picket went back into the house.

"Melissa. We are back. Would you like to sit down?"

"What's going on?"

"We have just avoided what could have been a death experience for you, but we have to ask if you would wear a wire, and go on a date with Jeff."

"A wire? You are scaring me."

"We'll have plain clothes officers in the restaurant at tables in front and behind you."

"Is this to do with Sara?"

"How do you know Sara?"

"I am best friends with Sara and Jen, and they told me about him last night. I could hardly believe it, the Diamond Strangler. I've seen the news."

"Will you do it?"

"I-I am not sure…he could kill me…." Melissa shivered.

"Just like a regular date. Just ask him personal questions and appear to be interested. Keep an eye on the time, and tell him you are going to sleep over at a friend's place."

Pickett went outside to bring in the wire for Melissa to wear.

"Also, we need permission to put surveillance equipment in your bedroom, and enter your house; sign here."

***

It was 5, Melissa and law enforcement arrived in the Edge Bar. Jeff approached Melissa and sat down. The lighting was low.

"You seem a little nervous, Melissa."

"Always am when meeting new people."

"Okay, let's order drinks."

"Jeff, tell me a little about you?"

"Well, am mostly on my own. I am wealthy beyond normal, and I like women in the 30's."

"Why?"

"Because once I was ready to settle down, but she ditched me for another man."

"That must have been hard."

"Yes, difficult to get her out of my mind even though it was months ago. You are a lot like her, my type. Now, it is my turn. Have you ever met someone you fell in love with at first sight?"

"No, I have not dated much."

"No boyfriends on your social media, at least."

Melissa took a breath, a hard breath but kept going.

"What is your last name, Jeff, so I can look at your profile? Turnabout is fair play."

A lady came around. "You are a cute couple, a picture perhaps?"

"Sure, why not. I'll pay," said Melissa.

Jeff seemed startled, "Maybe another day."

"Just one of me then." The woman did get him in the photo, but only part of his face. "Why so camera shy?"

"Just don't like that."

Melissa could see he was agitated.

"Let's talk about us," he said. He grabbed her hand as she tried to draw it away, but he held onto it. "You are very beautiful."

Melissa tried to keep her composure but he said, "Some die a little bit from such composure." He laughed. "You have a nice neckline also."

He moved over to her side of the table, and put his hands around her neck.

She tried not to jump right out of her skin.

"Can I come over to your house? I have a rather large gun in my pocket."

Two police officers came over posing as friends. "Hi, Melissa."

"These are my friends, Jeff."

"Ready to go?"

"Sure am. I am going to their place tonight."

"Oh!?!"

"It was nice to meet you, Jeff," and Melissa added, "Can you cover the bill?"

"Yes."

She got up and shook his hand.

The waiter came around and asked for a bank card. He put cash on the table, and ordered more drinks for himself.

Once in the unmarked car, Melissa said, "Oh God, that was just too real."

Matt and Pickett were in the front seat. Pickett was driving, and Matt said, "Thank you for your help. Now we'll get you somewhere safe."

Jeff thought to himself at the table. She's *perfect, but not for tonight. Tomorrow she'll be home. Plenty of time to make a sleeping beauty. Just drink a few more.*

He stayed until the bar closed unaware he was now the one being observed.

***

Sara met Matt at the Beacon for dinner. Matt had a thing for roses, but this time he presented her with a single rose.

"Thank-you, how goes the murder investigation?"

"We have a suspect, and that is all I can say. Is there an extra bed in your room?"

"Why would you need an extra bed? I thought you would like to share mine," she laughs.

"Your laugh is infectious."

"Yes, one does have to have a sense of humor. I don't suppose you wish to eat the fish? It is kinda like wearing the same old socks because you like them."

"What is wrong with my socks? They are standard issue." He rolls up his pant legs, and shows off his socks.

"Oh, I don't mind the fish."

"Socks are extra."

"I thought as much. What is the charge for taking them off?"

"I will tell you on the pier. Whisper it into your ear."

"So why the extra bed?"

"Melissa needs a place to stay. I understand you know each other?"

"Why, yes."

"We need to save police expenses where we can."

"Oh come on Matt. There is more to it than that. What gives?"

"Yes, you are right, my darling." He lifts her hand from the table and nibbles and kisses it. "Let's go for a walk on the pier while we wait for our meal. The waitress will come and get us when it is ready."

"Sounds like you do this often. Approximately, when do you take your socks off?"

The sun was glowing and sparkling on the water of the lake where a mountain is in sight: the mountain in the distance has two hills the shape of a woman's breasts. A soft wind blew Sara's red hair upwards and away from her face.

Matt had his hand in hers, and then he drew her close for a kiss. "I love you, Sara. My socks are yours."

She hugged and hugged him with a warm heart.

He whispered, "For you there is no charge."

\*\*\*

Sara, Jen, and Melissa sat on the beds in Sara's room the morning after Melissa had met the Diamond Strangler.

Sara and Jen said in unison, "We know you know something, out with it."

"Well, he's tall, brown hair and with a twist to his smile that makes him creepy. We had drinks."

"You went for a date?!!"

"Yes, it was the officer's idea."

"For God's sake," said Sara, "So, what happened?"

"He touched me. I almost jumped out of my skin, and to be honest, I have never dated a serial killer before that I know of."

"Where were you?"

"The Edge bar."

Jen nodded. "We need more information. We will have to go to the bar to get it."

Sara agreed. "Is there a bank card receipt? Fingerprints on a glass?"

They both looked at Melissa, "Do you have any money? We are going to have to bribe the bartender, and while we are there have a drink."

They pooled their resources putting money down on the beds.

"We know about the ghost bullet," said Sara to Melissa.

"What?"

Sara, Jen, and Melissa put themselves up near the bar, and ordered drinks.

"There was a man in here last night with this lady. What do you know of him?" asked Sara, laying extra money on the bar.

"No need for the money, lady. He has been in here before, and has dated a number of women. He stayed until closing, and left with Cindy, she's a regular around here."

"What did the police find out?" asked Jen.

"I think they put a tail on him. Not much, he wiped his glass, the table, and chair clean with a napkin. He paid in cash. And then the police, some of them, were gone with this lady." He pointed to Melissa.

The bartender put on the news. There was a picture of a woman there with the caption running along the bottom of the page "...is this the latest dead victim of the Diamond Strangler? Do you know this woman?"

"Oh no," said to the bartender, "It's Cindy."

Melissa turned to face Sara and Jen, "It could have been *me*."

Back at police headquarters, Matt was going ballistic. "What do you mean you lost him? This is now on us. We could have prevented her death."

Pickett was explaining for the men, "The tail lost him. He's good. He caught on fast. What we do know is that he has had training on this. The men know what the stakes are."

"I have to explain this to Frank, and Frank is not going to be happy about it. It means another conference with the media, and Frank doesn't like having to report up the chain of command that we lost one on our own watch."

Pickett added, "We had four cars on him with close radio contact. Two cars were parallel, one in back and it took us a while trying to get a car out in front. He raced out ahead: we couldn't get the car in front of him. He knew the side streets, and took a lot of back alleys. They followed protocol. We think he dodged us in some underground parking."

"Damn," said Matt.

"Crap is right," said Pickett, "I hate more than anything giving the family a death notification."

"See about video footage around her building and underground parking. We have to put this guy close to the crime scene."

***

Matt met Sara, Jen, and Melissa for an early breakfast at 7 am the next morning. He didn't call the meeting. They did.

The place made some nice eggs and hash browns and coffee. Matt questioned, "What is this about?"

Jen sat uncomfortably in a chair, "...It's about the bullet, and the bar. We would like to share information. You start."

"He got away last night."

"He left with Cindy."

"How do you know that?"

"We all bought drinks from the bartender at the Edge, said Sara.

"I will send Picket to see the bartender."

"And now to the bullet," said Jen with Sara holding her hand.

"We have a bullet," said Jen.

"What bullet? You withheld evidence?"

"The one I dug out of my door frame when Jeff shot at me." Look, it has no serial number. We, me and Sara researched it, a ghost bullet." Jen handed him the bullet by passing it along the table to him. "I didn't mean to. I gave it to Sara. Too much shock."

"I know that he killed her," blurted Melissa.

"What?"

"He touched me. When I touch people or things I get images like a movie for a while." Melissa's eyes were clear.

"We can't use that as evidence, and you know that you two could be charged. I will have to run this by Frank upstairs. Is there anything now that I don't know?"

"–yes, there is," said Sara. "He frequents the bar."

***

After Matt left the restaurant, Sara, Jen, and Melissa stayed behind.

Melissa said, "I could have told him more, Sara."

"What do you mean?"

"I get a motion picture in my head, Jen. Kinda of like when you go back to an event in your mind and play it forward?"

"How do you do it?"

"It started at university. I studied hard using a dictionary. Learning what words I did not know, I could see the textbook and flip the pages in it while doing the exam. Then it took a turn when the teacher touched me, and I learned he thought I was cheating, but he couldn't prove it. I didn't."

"That's a photographic memory," said Sara.

"It's more. When I touch someone I can walk in their shoes for a bit. I had difficulty turning it off at first."

"I think it is terrible. They didn't catch the bastard," said Sara. "What do you think Jen?"

"We need to track him. Can you turn it back on, Melissa?"

"You know, those trackers you can get at the High Tech Gremlin's High Tech on 10th," said Jen.

"Sure, let's Google it on my phone. Here. The price is $49.00/month, cancel any time, and it's good for a long range, and has a 60 minute listen-in feature," said Sara. "Problem is we will have to bolt it in."

"Gremlin's, here we come. Thank God for shopping, for some crazy glue and for some heavy duty magnets. You know this is illegal?"

Dead silence.

Then Jen added, "They track us all the time with cookies. Imagine that, something we would enjoy eating. Try cameras on every corner and who knows what else."

"I don't know if I can turn it back on. He scares me. Is the device accessible by phone?"

"Yes. Says it has an emergency responders list. Maybe we should put Matt and Pickett on there?" asked Jen.

"I will ask Matt for Pickett's cell number. I already have his."

Matt was back at the police station reviewing all the evidence coming in.

"We found something."

"What? A hair? You found lots, Pickett?"

"Something more juicy."

"Okay, what?"

"DNA Saliva."

Matt perked up in his chair.

"It's male."

"Did you have a chance to run it through the database?"

"Yes, still processing."

"Pickett what else do we have?"

"A fingernail that has no nail polish on it. I hope that nails the coffin shut on him."

"Right. And?"

"Nothing on the car yet, I have zeroed the officers in on that one."

"Thanks. What would I ever do without you?"

"Crap, I don't know. By the way, happy birthday!" Pickett pulls a cup cake out of his office drawer, and places it on Matt's desk, and lights a candle. "They never said this job was going to be easy."

"Can you cut the crap?"

They both laughed.

"No one said we were too fat to eat cup cakes either, did they? Matt looked around at his fellow officers. "It all goes in the crapper, right Pickett?"

Pickett picked up the phone. "They found the car? Great. In a car park? No, where? Right outside?"

"He's taunting us. We have spent hours looking for that car. Which clever police officer found it? Promote the bastard. Give him a FREE cup cake, Pickett. My turn to say crap."

"Another dead body inside the car, double crap."

\*\*\*

Sara said, "We're a team!"

"Yes."

"Yes."

"Melissa? What do you need to turn your gift back on?"

"Jen, let me touch you. I really don't know. I have just spent more time turning it off."

Jen gave Melissa her hands.

"It is a bit like spying, Sara, and I always feel guilty about that. It is rather like sitting in a room listening to wind chimes. I like them so I say to the universe in my mind how wonderful they are, and then there is this annoyance report that comes out of nowhere. Only once have I had it confirmed, what I sensed, when a woman came to my door upset because her neighbor wanted the wind chimes taken down. She knocked at my actual door and said so."

"Now that is profound, don't you think Jen?"

"Yeah."

"Spooky," Jen said.

"Jen, you have been really concerned for your family, and about the bullet. Yesterday you moved about the apartment back and forth. Baby Kevin? He's crying. Moving forward I see that you have been found by Jeff. He knows you are in the here. I can see him."

"Oh, my God. Sara?"

"What about me?"

Melissa touched Sara. "Oh no, I see him strangling you."

"We must do something," said Sara, feeling a strange sensation on her neck.

Jen asked, "Does it work with just people or objects too?"

"What about dead bodies?"

"I have never tried on a dead person before."

"We have to go to the morgue," said Sara, "To find out!"

***

Matt and Pickett are looking over the female dead body in the front of the car outside the police station.

"This is a change in MO," said Matt.

"Agreed."

"There is the red shoe."

"And there is a note," said Pickett, reading out loud, "So you think you can catch me. Someone close to you will die."

"Sara? Jen? My mother?" said Matt.

"Seems, we'd better cover our bases on family…. This bastard is watching even now."

"Pickett, tell the others everything. There is car insurance in the vehicle, but the car's license plate does not match."

"This means there are potentially two murder scenes. Send a team out there right now?"

"Yes, and send details to cover our families in the city. Seems he doesn't keep the same vehicle; so, we'll also have to keep an eye out for stolen cars."

"It is a long shot, but patrol has to be made aware he's carrying a loaded gun."

***

"Distract him, Jen. We have to get Melissa into the morgue," said Sara.

"I want to puke," said Melissa, "The smell is awful. Mothballs don't begin to cover it. The smell is overpowering."

Jen approached the front desk in the morgue, and cried to the only person there that she had taken a fall off her high heel shoes. Sara and Jen hid around the corner and waited.

"I am so sorry, and I can't walk very well. Can you show me to First Aid?"

"He complied. Wow," whispered Melissa.

"Good. We go in."

Sara and Melissa enter the room where two bodies are on separate tables.

"I don't know which one to touch, and I don't like this."

"Just touch one."

Melissa just closed her eyes, and touched a body. "Yes, he's feeling a sense of morbid satisfaction. This is Cindy. She's very cold. I can still see him in the Edge bar. There is a movie, and then it goes dark."

"Now, the next one."

Melissa opened her eyes, "This body is still warm. He's laughing, and there is definitely another body, too. He likes what he does. He likes it."

"Can you process two at once?"

"I am overwhelmed. It is too much. Too many pictures."

"Okay, just try to take it in slower."

"I can't. I have to shut it down."

"Maybe later you can sort it out. Let's get out of here."

***

Matt and Pickett were looking over new evidence.

Matt sighed and took a sip of his coffee, "The Saliva?"

"The guy is our system, Joe Wright. His picture does not match Jeff from the bar. Wright has a rap sheet for everything including robbery."

"We still have to check up on him. And the finger nail?"

"Could be Jeff's. Still unidentified, but male."

"We need a sketch of this Jeff. We have to get some traction on these cases. There have been too many murders."

"Matt, more detectives and other resources are on their way. Checked with Frank this morning, and he has authorized it."

Matt knew he was facing a lot of pressure to find this guy, and Pickett was always there to have his back.

"Get Melissa and Jen in here to see the sketch artists. Bring in Sara as well. Do we have their fingerprints too? It would help to rule them out of the cases."

\*\*\*

Sara, Jen, and Melissa arrived at the police station.

As they walked in, Pickett was answering some question about a note, "Fingerprint matches."

Sara whispered to Jen and Melissa, "Melissa, you can find out what they know. Can you touch them?"

Melissa nodded. She shook two separate handshakes holding them for an extra few minutes after using the hand sanitizer on the desk. She was shown to the sketch artist and moved down the hall to the first door on the right.

Matt turned to Jen, "Did you see who fired the bullet at you?"

"Yes, but only for a few minutes."

Pickett showed her to the second room on the right.

Jen complied.

So Sara was left there with Matt. "How are you feeling?"

"Well, we can't go home. He's loose out there, and I can't shake the feeling he knows where we are."

"I get it."

"He was bold enough to be in my house with me in it."

"Do you have any leads?"

"Yes, and there is a lot of evidence to process. It all takes time. Sara, he said taking her hands in his, "I understand it has been hard to deal with, but I have a small gift for you and the other ladies."

"What is it?"

"Over dinner?" he snuck a kiss.

Pickett returned and Sara blushed. "Can I come too?"

"Pick you up at 7-ish?"

"Sure," she smiled.

Pickett chimed in. "What a lucky man you are. Sara, come with me. You can stay in our lounge with a modern magazine. Your friends will be a while."

An hour or so later, Sara looked up and through the window where Matt and Pickett were. Matt waved her in. Pickett handed him the sketches. He showed them to all three women.

Jen said, "Melissa's is the best. It's him."

And then Sara in an upset voice, "That's him! He was at the resort last night. He was outside the room. I went to get ice with the dog in tow. That's him in Melissa's picture."

"Pickett, get these pictures to Frank. He has to make an announcement to the press. Follow it with an APB."

"We have two choices regarding these women and their security: one, leave them where they are with extra guards outside their rooms, or move them to a more secure location," said Pickett, "Your call, Matt."

***

Back at the resort, Jen went to pick up her stuff and put it in a suitcase. Her husband had left a written note on the table, "Kevin and I are at the park with the dog."

Beside it was another note in hand writing she didn't recognize, and it read, "Give the diamond and the red shoe to Melissa. It is in your closet."

Jen screamed, and ran next door to Sara's. She panicked dialing 911.

Matt and Pickett arrived at the resort 10 minutes later.

"He's probably watching from where?"

Matt said, "I suggest we move the women by heli to our second location. Sara said they didn't touch anything."

"Since he was here, and we have the time as 8:00 pm, I'll check for video," said Pickett.

Melissa and Jen were sitting there in Sara's room. Sara petted the dog. He provided a little comfort.

"You okay?" asked Matt.

"Yes," said Melissa "The others are in turmoil."

"We will both make the arrangements for a new location."

Melissa sat on the bed with her eyes on the dog. It had been a very busy day to the morgue, to the sketch artist and now this. She wanted to cry, but couldn't. It was a very strange feeling. *Why did I have to tell them my gift? I don't want to see these things.* She shut it all off in her head.

*** 

"The phone lines are gonna ring now, Pickett. Matt sat at his desk, and munched on some celery. "Apparently eating celery makes me more attractive to the opposite sex."

Pickett laughed. "Frank did an excellent job with the media. The paper printed the picture front page with a big heading, "The Diamond Strangler. Social media is buzzing with it."

The phone rang, a woman's voice…."Hello? Detective Pickett here. What's he look like?"

"Like the guy in your picture. He drove up in a blue car."

"License plate number?"

Pickett handed the number to Matt who looked in the database. "It's a stolen car. Reported yesterday. Could be him."

"249 Cherry Street. That's my address. He went in to the house next door. My name is Carol."

"Can you wait for us outside? Be there in 10 minutes."

Pickett looked at Matt, "Is there a car tracker in the trunk? We will take one or two cars?"

"Two."

***

Sara, Jen, and Melissa settled at their new location across town and not far from the airport. The helicopter ride took them over the city's tall buildings and streets.

"Ok, Melissa. Jen and I would like to know what you found out."

Jen nodded and leaned forward. Melissa was crying. "Well, the two women in the morgue saw him up to the last minute. He immobilized them with rope on their hands and feet. When he was pulling the rope out of his jacket, he dropped a driver's license on the carpet. I looked at it, but did not get all the numbers. The numbers in the middle were 3654. The license looks like it is not local. I can't get any more than that."

Sara and Jen tried to comfort her.

Sara said softly,"What is it?"

"I watch them die," Melissa sobbed. "The print on the name is small. Jeff Bro-."

"It's okay, Melissa. Thank-you. We will have Matt run it through the computer by telling him a story? What shall we make up, won't we Sara?"

***

Matt and Pickett went to check out the lead at Carol's place which was also in the Marpole area.

She met them at her front door, and began to describe in more detail the man she saw. "Brown hair. Beady eyes. Wicked grin. Truly him."

"How far away were you?" asked Matt.

"Oh, maybe 30 feet."

Both Matt and Pickett could hardly control their laughter.

"And did you wear glasses?"

"No, I didn't have them on." She pointed to the next door house.

They went to the front door and knocked, "Police."

It was a little unnerving not knowing what would happen next and to be prepared for anything.

The door opened and a woman stood in the doorway. "What can I do for you?"

"We are just doing a safety check. Can you step outside so we can talk?" said Matt.

"Is there anyone else here?"

"None of your business, but I brought a man home from the bar last night."

"Can you come and stand over here while we talk to him?"

"Sure. What's his name?"

"Hell I don't know…. I think it's Darren."

"We just want to have a chat with him."

"Darren? Can you step outside, please?"

"Darren, which car did you drive up in?"

"That one."

"Let's walk over there."

"Is this your car?"

"Well, no."

"Whose car is it?"

"Okay, I stole it, but the guy didn't need it." He looked at the ground.

"Which guy?"

"Jeff, I steal them for him."

"What does Jeff look like? Like this?" Matt pulled out a photocopy of the sketch.

"Yeah, that's him."

"Would you be willing to talk to us at the station about Jeff?"

"Sure, but he's a customer. I won't give the info for free."

"We can talk about that when we get there." Matt put Darren in the back of the police cruiser.

Pickett radioed. "Yes, almost done here, Matt."

"Pickett, did you give her the first degree about the serial killer? And a picture?"

"Sure. Code 21." (In police chatter that meant "dumb as beans"). Pickett jumped into his car.

*** 

In interrogation room "B" Matt sat across from Darren. Pickett was watching from behind glass.

"Darren, can I offer you a drink?"

"Yes, some of the hard stuff. "No...I guess you can't offer that." Darren was watching him.

"You can leave at any time, but I want you to hear me out. Okay?"

Darren looked down at his hands on the steel table. He nodded. "Yes, are you going to arrest me? Handcuffs?"

"No, I am interested in another matter. What do you know about this Jeff?"

"Oh, you mean twisty face."

"Yes."

"Is he the guy in the photocopy I showed you? Same one?"

"Yes, he has money, and lots of it. I get cars for him very regularly."

"Do you have a standard place where he picks up the cars from you?"

"Why would I tell you?"

"We would like your help."

"Do you think you could let us know when he calls you and where he's going to meet you?"

"What's in it for me? He could kill me."

"Witness protection and new ID, Darren, women are dying."

There was a long pause. Matt could see he would have to wait for an answer.

"Any money?"

"You would get some help there too including finding other work if you want it."

"I want no women on my conscience. A serial killer?"

"Yes, the police have not seen anything like this. He's not going to stop. His targets have been women; we feel the woman he dated last night could have been one of them."

"He calls me every few days lately."

"Did he give you a number to call?"

"No. It was always caller unknown."

"Could this be a win/win deal for you? You do realize that you could be next when he has no further use for you. You have seen him."

Darren sat upright. "Yes...deal."

"Then protective custody will start now."

***

Matt picked up Sara for their romantic dinner date later that evening at the Beacon. He had phoned ahead to his manager to ask for her assistance in buying some chocolates. He made small chat with Sara in the car and then sat her down in an ornate wooden chair.

"I know we are not going to have fish in your uniformed socks tonight. Matt."

"You look ravishing."

"Lol!"

"Yes, I was hoping to take your mind off of things, but there is a pressing matter to discuss," said Matt. "Let's eat first." He kissed her hand and looked into those blues.

The meal passed quickly. Mostly, with what Sara wanted in a relationship. Matt was listening. He already knew a lot about her. No criminal record, and that she managed her own digital marketing business.

"You are a bit preoccupied, Matt?" She put her fork down.

"Yes. There is the small matter of the morgue."

Sara took a deep breath in, and had some water to wash it down.

"The matter is somewhat serious–the tampering of evidence. We have you three on video. The mortician was mortified."

"But–"

"But what? Why were you women there, Sara. Melissa was touching dead bodies. What the hell for?"

"Melissa has a gift."

"You are joking, right?"

"No, I'm not." Sara closed her arms over her chest.

"Tell me. You don't believe in this psychic mumbo jumbo."

"It's not like that!" Sara had tears welling up. She started to cry. "If you are going to handcuff me, just take me and leave the others out of it."

"Sara, I am not going to press charges; just tell me what you were doing in there."

"Melissa has a photographic memory; that is what helped with the sketch."

"Okay. Breathe now. Deep breath."

"When she touches people she sees and hears like a movie."

"And what does this have to do with dead bodies?"

"Everything! We thought we could help you with evidence. We found something or Melissa did."

"So, you thought you could solve the cases?"

"This is dangerous, Sara."

"The numbers were 3654."

"You must never go near this guy. I don't want to lose you. I love you, Sara. Please say you won't."

"Will you check the numbers? Melissa thinks it is from ID. You will have to talk to Melissa about what she saw."

"Okay, Sara, but I don't hold out much hope for that. You have broken the chain of evidence. We will need your DNA and fingerprints. What did Melissa touch?"

"Just two arms."

"Which ones?"

"The right ones."

"Tomorrow you and the others will come into the office and receive a stern reprimand. Now, let's enjoy the rest of our evening. Remember, I promised you a gift for each of you?"

"Yes."

He took out a small box and gave it to Sara. Inside was a heart-shaped necklace. He put it around her neck, and then the manager came with 12-stemmed red roses and chocolates.

"It's beautiful. They are beautiful."

He then gave her a very long kiss.

Matt and Frank are in Frank's office with Sara, Jen, and Melissa in the late afternoon.

"Matt tells me you have been up to mischief with the law. He also tells me that you have given some numbers which may or may not relate to the murder investigation through some hocus-pocus."

"Yes, sir," said Matt.

"Because of this, and because we now have to run the numbers, is there any additional information that you as the public wish to give?"

"Yes, it may be a California state driver's license," said Melissa.

"Thank-you. Now, to the other matter at hand, we can because of your actions have all three of you charged, but Matt says you have agreed to stay clear of this police matter. Stay away from this Jeff?"

"Yes," said Sara.

"All of you will be placed in a holding cell for 24 hours at least and be given food and water. Legally, we can hold you for 24. I suggest you keep your word in future because I will not be so polite the next time you are here in my office. Matt, fingerprint them and get their DNA, of course with their consent. Matt, escorted them out of the office, and after processing, put them in a holding cell and slammed the door shut."

Pickett nabbed him in the hall. "Darren has received a call from Jeff. Yesterday, I took Darren down to the impound lot, and Darren picked out a car that Jeff would like. Darren says he has one hour to deliver."

Pickett and Matt are called into Frank's office, "I have been reviewing the cases files, and you have a Mr. Wright here with DNA saliva found at the scene of one of the murders."

"He seems to have been there," said Matt.

"We haven't looked into that yet, Sir."

"Why not? Act on it. The pressure is mounting to find this guy. There have been three murders so far. The mayor isn't happy. This should be an open and shut case. Bring Mr. Wright in."

"On it, Sir," said Matt, and out the door they went.

Frank yelled after them, "Results, gentlemen."

As Matt passed by his desk on the way to the car, there was a note on his desk. The note said Darren was in the lobby.

Pickett pulled out some car keys out of his pocket, and shook them, "Keys for an auto Darren will drive to the meet Jeff."

Darren arrived at Pickett's desk, "One question or maybe two, Darren. Have you ever been to the Edge bar?"

"How did you know? I will deliver to Jeff near there this time."

"What instructions did Jeff give you?"

"I gave other cars to Jeff. He leaves the car before I drop off the next car. He puts the money in the last car, and I put the keys. I don't even see him at all. Sometimes I walk into the bar and sit there. I watched him a couple of times, so I know who he is."

"What do you do with the cars he returns to you?" asked Matt.

"I have my own impound lot."

"Do we have a tracker on the car, Pickett?"

Pickett smiled, "Yes, we are all set."

Matt turns to the room of his fellow officers, "Darren's protective detail will follow him. I need two officers to follow and track the guy that gets into the car that Darren will be driving. Just track. You know the drill."

"Darren, we need the address of the lot. Some of those vehicles are involved in a crime scene."

Darren reluctantly agreed, "Full protection, right?"

Matt called over Darren's protective detail, "Follow Darren and if shots are fired, protect him. After that, drive him to the lot and have him point out which cars Jeff drove. Get forensics out there. The lot of you head out to the area of the Edge bar."

"Aren't you coming?" asked Darren nervously.

"No, you are in good hands."

"Good luck and happy hunting, boys. Keep me or Pickett posted on the radio."

***

Matt and Pickett got into their unmarked car, and drove to Wright's house. They get to the door and identify themselves, and the door opens.

"Are you Mr. Wright?"

"Yes."

"I am Matt and this is Pickett. We are from homicide. Nothing about your family, but we would like to ask you some questions. Would you mind coming down to the station?"

"Sure, what's it about?"

"We will explain when we get there," said Pickett.

"You are not under arrest, Mr. Wright, and we will bring you home afterward. We can see you have a naked young lady tied up in the living room."

"Oh, yes. I will be fine once I am out of these knots. I really don't mind as it is rather kinky."

Pickett untied her. She put on some clothes. "We think, young lady, you should come, too," said Matt.

"I'll just get my purse."

In interrogation room "B" Pickett sits with Mr. Wright. Matt watches through a one-way mirror. Frank joins him.

"Now, we have to show you a few scenes that are very graphic. The women are dead, and we have to ask you how you are connected with these cases." Pickett takes out the various photos and put them in front of Mr. Wright. Each women strangled around the neck; each with a bullet in the skull.

"Connected?"

"It seems your DNA Saliva is on one of those bodies. You realize, Mr. Wright this is very serious. Your DNA was found at a crime scene."

Mr. Wright was visibly shaken, but did not respond.

"You realize Mr. Wright this is what we call an open and shut case. We have the DNA evidence, and we can charge you with at least one crime, and we can do that now."

Mr. Wright was wringing his hands, but remained silent.

"The saliva is yours, Mr. Wright. How did it get there?"

He shook his head and said, "I am not giving you a thing."

Pickett studied Mr. Wright. He was thin, brown hair. Age 52. His eyes darted to the left. He probed further, "You know if you don't say anything in your defense because of the evidence, I will be bumping this up to the DA for formal charges?"

Mr. Wright blinked and sat up in his chair, "I want a lawyer."

"It is your right, sir. Your saliva was on a dead woman's body. Do you know this woman?" Pickett points out the picture and pushes it forward.

Mr. Wright's face flushed, but he never said another word. In handcuffs, an officer took him to holding.

***

Next, the young woman was brought into interrogation room "B".

Just a few questions, Miss?"

"July."

"We brought you here to check on your safety. How old are you?"

"19," she smiled.

"How well do you know Mr. Wright?"

"We just met at the Edge bar a few weeks back, and have been dating. He's very kinky, yes…."

"How so?"

"I don't want to say, except he ties me up and then tastes my body."

"Do you know this man?" Pickett put in front of her the picture of Jeff.

"Yes, he sometimes watches."

"Okay, Miss July. We advise you to steer clear of Mr. Wright and this Jeff until homicide sorts out the matter.

"Jeff likes to put bullets on my body and roll them."

Pickett laid out the homicide pictures. "Do you know any of these women?"

"Yes, that is Cindy from the bar! She's...dead?"

"Yes."

"Oh, no, the Diamond Strangler?"

"You shouldn't go home now. We think you should stay in a hotel for a few days. Wait here a moment."

Matt and Pickett confer outside.

"He was not helpful," said Pickett. "I can't put my finger on it, but there is something up with him."

"Yes, maybe he was in on at least one killing. Maybe he loves the taste of death, Matt."

"Or maybe he just loves to taste."

\*\*\*

Sara, Jen, and Melissa were sitting in a cell.

"What are we going to do?" asked Sara.

"We have to find a way to put Jeff behind bars," said Jen.

Silence.

"I know where Jeff likes to haunt," said Melissa.

Matt dropped by with three cups of coffee, "Jail cell service." He kidded them. "How are you doing?"

Sara answered, "The handcuffs you put us in were stone cold to wear, and when the cell door closed, all I could think of was a feeling of wanting so bad to escape."

"Melissa, we ran the numbers that you gave us for the California ID. There are a lot of names on that list. Can you narrow it down? A birth date?"

Melissa sat on the cell bed with her hands touching the itchy grey blanket. Her brown eyes looked like they were somewhere else. Slowly, she reviewed the tape in her head. Yes, October 10, 1978. "I thought you didn't believe me."

"Sara says you have a gift. I thought about it. I have a photographic memory which comes in handy with my job, but I am still unsure how yours differs from mine. He smiled. "We have to chase up every lead. With the additional manpower and budget, we can do just that. It is now a manhunt."

"We would still like to help, Matt," said Sara.

Jen nodded.

Melissa replied, "I know where he likes to haunt."

"Where?"

"The Edge bar."

"The bartender, remember?" said Jen.

"Okay."

"The bartender said he comes in there."

Pickett joined them at the cell.

"Have the boys run this DOB October 10, 1978, and meet me at the desk. We are going for a ride to the Edge bar after all."

***

Pickett drove Matt in the car which was the custom on Fridays. It wasn't far away, so within 5 minutes they were there. Darren was placing the keys into the impound vehicle for delivery to Jeff, and was back in the police car.

"There's our guy, Pickett."

Jeff was looking around. His eyes were shifting, darting around as if looking for trouble. He crossed the street and got into the car, and pulled out into traffic. The boys followed at a safe distance.

Pickett and Matt walked into the bar and ordered two tall drinks, one a Shirley Temple, and the other a tomato juice with a piece of celery. They asked the waitress to call the bartender to the table.

"We have a few questions to ask you," said Matt.

Pickett showed ID. "Do you know any of the men in these photos, and this artist's sketch?"

"This guy in the sketch is Jeff. He left the bar with Cindy, the other guy is Mr. Wright, who was also here sitting at another table."

"Anything else?"

"Yes, Jeff was just in here a few minutes ago. I had a difficult time serving him because of Cindy."

"If you see him again, don't directly look at him too much. Just find a place where you can call us where he cannot see you doing it. Don't approach him with any of this, okay?"

Matt and Pickett then left the bar.

***

The two uniformed officers, tracking…. Jeff raced… to catch up to him.

Jeff got out of the car near Shoe Haven and peered in their window. The store was empty. He had no window of opportunity, *yet*. Perhaps he should look elsewhere today. Perhaps he could call his buddy Mr. Wright. He called, but there was no answer.

He walked back to his car after doing some shopping at the local grocery market. *Maybe he wouldn't pay cash this time*, but the up-to-date camera system told him otherwise.

He thought over his pretty ladies, and appreciated his moments with them, seeing their eyes, their lips, their fingernails. He looked down at his own nails. One was broken. *Time to get a manicure.*

He pulled out and drove to a shop, walked in and waited for the manicurist to call. *Maybe he could ask her out on a date she would no longer remember the day after.*

The two officers logged every place he went including a high-end residence on Queens Street. They typed in the address to find out who owned the place, Mr. & Mrs. Braeston. Pictures came up on their dashboard computer. Matt ordered them to stay put. In the morning, Pickett and Matt made an appearance near the house.

Jeff came out of the house, and collecting the mail, threw it inside. The officers followed him.

After he left, Matt and Picket canvassed the neighbor next door.

"Hello, Miss?"

"Just call me, Julie."

She was an older woman in her 80's.

Pickett flashed a badge.

"We are doing a neighbor check. Have you seen Mr. or Mrs. Braeston?

"Actually, they are normally out and about, come to think of it, I haven't seen them in weeks. Their son, Jeff? Came over, and introduced himself. He said they were on an extended world tour."

"Have you met Jeff before? Is this him." Matt showed his picture.

"Well—yes, that's him."

"Okay, we are just concerned about them. Can we keep this between us? It is not wise to say anything to Jeff yet."

Matt checked his computer in the car. "Do Mr. & Mrs. Braeston have a son? "

"No, there were no children on file."

Pickett said, "I'll go round the back, and I'll meet you in the front. Going to scout out the neighborhood."

Ten minutes later, Pickett arrived back. "I looked into the yards and there was nothing to see, but there is a vacant lot about a block down we should check out."

"Nothing out of the ordinary here," said Matt.

"I think we should check the vacant lot too."

"Matt and Pickett drove the car over to the lot which was surrounded by trees. A creek ran on the property. There was a small path leading down underneath a mound. Inside, walking on the dirt with their flashlights on, they found a human bone, a jaw.

"We are going to have to get a forensics team down here in stealth mode. Give a cover story to the neighbors and the media."

Matt had this feeling that Jeff has been really busy. *A body dump? Completely different case?* Pickett was stone cold silent too. In either case, the department's budget was shot for this year. More detectives would be needed, and he felt sorry for the jaw, for everything.

When they got back to the car, they sat there stunned.

"Get me Frank on the blower. Frank? We think we found more dead bodies. Send an unmarked car, no sirens to our location," said Pickett.

"We want to call Jeff in for an interview. The problem is we have very little to go on, and after he gets out of the 24 hours he may flee," said Matt.

"Agreed, what do you need? The rest of the team and surveillance is listening."

"Where is he now?"

"Down at the beach. He's eating sardines, carrots, and celery for lunch. Lots of people down here."

"SWAT standing by."

***

Matt and Pickett arrived at the beach seeing SWAT parked a block away, and the two officers standing 15 feet from Jeff. They walked over to SWAT while talking to them all with buds in their ears.

"Okay, so did he finish his sardines?" Matt said sarcastically.

"Are we going to arrest him?" said Pickett.

"No, we are not absolutely sure, but he's stalking and killing women, and we have to do something. Maybe we can hold him for an illegal gun. We have to try and keep him off the street."

The SWAT Commander here! How do you want to do this?"

"Pickett and I will flank him by sneaking up on him. If we can't take him down, and he shoots, you have my authorization to shoot back. Wound him only, please."

Jeff got up from sitting on the beach, and walked down to the pier. He was looking around and smiling. It was as if the bastard knew they were there.

Matt and Pickett walked out onto the pier, flanking him. He said, "Hello, very politely, and raised a gun over his head and took a shot, a bullet tore through the air faster than a seagull could fly: a seagull dropped to the ground, dead.

SWAT moved in and took their shot.

Jeff fell to his knees grasping his left arm. His gun bounced and shot again and skidded across the wooden planks into the drink. "What took you so long? I've been waiting for you."

Matt and Pickett got him fully to ground, and put the cuffs on him.

***

Pickett took Jeff to a holding cell, the one next door to Sara, Jen, and Melissa. He pushed Jeff inside steel bars and heard metal on metal close the door. He was in the same cell as Mr. Wright.

Mr. Wright spat between the bars, and Jeff yelled at him, "What the hell? What are you doing here you little f**k? You didn't return my call."

Sara whispered to Melissa and Jen. *"Melissa, if you have the opportunity would you touch them? We need to know."*

"Hey, pretty ladies. What ya in for?" Jeff came over touching the bars and putting his hand outside his cell and around a wall into their cell. "Sweet, pretty lady, did you get the red shoe and the diamond?"

Melissa cringed, "I did, darling. Give me your hand." She massaged it, but she couldn't talk; the emotion was too strong. He kept talking but that did not matter. *"I had a girl once, but she betrayed me just like you will,"* he echoed in her mind.

He grabbed her hand, and then let go. "I'll get to you my pretty."

"So you think your buddy would like me then?"

"Mr. Wright wandered over and put his hand through the bars, "Darling, I am such a good lover compared to him."

"What the–. You always come across that way. I am gonna pound the crap out of you." He hit Mr. Wright on the side of the head. He fell to his knees with a second blow to the belly. "I will deal with you later. Just remember that."

Sara and Jen turned to see Melissa on her knees holding her belly. "I can't break the connection. There's too much pain."

"Wow, you feel his pain?"

"Yes, the punches."

"Look, Sara, she's developing bruises," said Jen.

"Oh, no."

"It's strong. The pain is subsiding. Never felt this before."

Sara and Jen steadied her as she tried to stand. Melissa made her way to the cell bed. "I'm out."

Pickett arrived with Mr. Wright's lawyer.

"Mr. Wright I see that you are injured. Do you wish to press charges against the police?" Mr. Wright was taken out of the cell.

"Pickett, can we get a glass of water for Melissa?"

"Sure thing."

"Are you alright?" asked Pickett.

"Yes, she'll be fine," said Sara.

***

Matt and Pickett sat down with Jeff in interrogation room "B" with Frank watching on.

"We know you were in some of the murders, Jeff. With Mr. Wright? Let us talk about that," commanded Matt.

Jeff smiled. He arched a sly brow. His denim blue eyes gave a hint. 'Let's play a game.

"Did you kill anyone?"

He laughed.

"No, I did not." His eyes darted. His eyelids went down and he shrugged.

Matt put the pictures on the table, one by one. "Let's start with these."

"Nope," he glared back. "Hell may freeze over first. Yes, they are pretty, aren't they?"

Matt didn't even blink, "What about those bodies on the lot?"

"Which one?"

"Do you mean there is more than one?"

"Are you admitting to these crimes?"

"No, not even one, I was pulling your leg. What do you mean dragging Joe Public in here?"

Matt was hot under the collar, but kept his cool. Pickett spoke, "You, as a concerned citizen, would not mind giving us your DNA and fingerprints, right?"

Jeff sneered. "This is when I lawyer up. All you guys can do is the paperwork," he mocked.

Matt folded up his file, "Lawyers are there to protect the innocent, Jeff, so are we."

Before he put Jeff back in a holding cell, Matt looked at his ID. He had two separate identities; one was from California that was the one that specified the birth date and numbers Melissa gave.

It was time to talk further with Melissa. He and Pickett were not going to let him get away with this.

They both walked down the corridor with Jeff to his new cell: it was time to release the girls as well.

"Melissa can I see you in my office?" enquired Matt.

"Us too!" chimed in Sara.

"Sure you too."

They all sat down on the comfortable couch in the office. Pickett and Matt got the desk chairs.

"Melissa, your story about the driver's license checked out." Matt put the driver's licenses on the desk in front of Melissa.

Melissa's eyes went wide. "So it is true then. Outside proof."

"We told you so," beamed Sara.

"Yes." Jen smiled.

"I have talked about it with Frank and Pickett. We feel you would be an asset to the department at this point. We would like to have your three as consultants. You would be sworn in and deputized."

"Really?"

"We would like your permission to give you these lockets. Sara has one, but there are ones for each of you. These contain a locater beacon and a microphone. We need your permission to activate them."

"You mean you were tracking me?" fretted Sara.

"No, you would have activated it only to call me if you were in trouble and you said you agreed, Sara."

"You didn't use it to spy on me?"

"No. Just press the side of the lockets to activate them."

Melissa had her eyes to the floor, "I don't know, Sara. This scares me and after what happened with the bruises, I don't know."

Melissa showed the bruises on the side of her face to Matt. They were mostly covered up by her hair.

"How did that happen?"

"Melissa reacted to both Jeff and Mr. Wright in the jail cell," said Jen.

"My gift seems to extend further than I thought. It seems that when Jeff struck Mr. Wright, I collapsed. I couldn't disconnect from the extreme emotion."

Jen reached out and held Melissa's hand. "Are we going to let him get away with this? I do understand, Melissa."

"You just don't know how much that hurt."

"Yes, but if we don't do this, Melissa, he's going to hurt another lady just like he was setting you up for."

There was a long pause before Melissa spoke. She raised her eyes up, "Yes, I will do it, but not without Sara and Jen."

"Good. It is all settled then," said Matt.

"We know you have a skill, Melissa," said Pickett curiously. "How would you do with bones?"

"Bones??"

*** 

Matt, Pickett, and the women met at the police station the following morning.

"There is gonna be a lot more of evidence," said Matt.

Pickett took the jaw bone out of the plastic bag; there was a hard sound as the jaw bone hit the table, and nearby papers rustled.

"All we know so far is that this jaw bone is male. The tech guys have taken what DNA they could. Problem is it will take 7-10 days to process. Melissa, could you touch the bone?"

Melissa reached, but then withdrew.

"Melissa please try," urged Jen.

She ran her fingers over the jaw, and over the teeth.

"What can you tell us?"

"This man was not expected to die. I can't tell you how recent. His name...last name is Brae–."

"Braeston?"

"Greg. He was standing by the door. I have never felt this way before. The jaw is very cold. He was knocked out."

"This we will confirm with forensics when we find the head that goes with the jaw. I just hope we find the rest of him. Meanwhile we will get dental records for the Braeston's," said Matt.

Melissa looked to the others as if she had seen a ghost. "I felt like there was another person there."

"Can you tell who it was?" asked Pickett.

"Can't tell who it was. It is just a feeling. He was tied up and woke back up on a brown dirt floor. That is all; that is all," she said hysterically. She said down on a chair like the weight of the thought was too much to bear."

"We are here with you Melissa," said Jen.

"We are all here."

"The images are dark, and it feels like the day of a solar eclipse where the figures are ghostly," she said. "Lost...."

*** 

Jeff was in his cell, chuckling to himself.

*I wonder why the pretty girls were here? Why they were in jail...the pretty girls. They won't find my past. I hid it all under the brown dirt. They won't find out.*

He chuckled some more.

He ran his hands over the bars.

He yelled incoherently into space, banging his hands on the cell door. "Where is my coffee?" *You won't find out about Ken. I needed the place. They were just inconvenient; both of them had to die.* "So what? My place. So what?"

***

Pickett and Matt were saddened by the fact that Mr. Wright had been released from the jail to await trial.

Mr. Wright stopped by to see the detectives. Gleefully, he stated he was Mr. Joe model citizen too, and was now in need of police protection.

"Why is that? Do you know Jeff?" said Matt.

"He'll kill me."

"So you do know him then."

"Yes," he snapped.

"We have no evidence, so we can't protect you," said Pickett. "If you come up with some, maybe we can talk about it." Pickett handed him a business card.

Mr. Wright sneered sucking his lips.

"It is up to you, but we advise you to do it soon."

Sara, Jen and Melissa were given a break for a while. They sat just having coffee with Matt and Pickett.

Melissa was trying to make sense of the images, "Matt, I am feeling disoriented. I don't have the actual scenes."

"We can remedy that." Matt pulled out the files and started with the first murder.

"Heavens, there are more? No wonder why. It's a jumble."

"It's okay. We will go through the evidence on each case file, piece by piece, including the other cold files we think may be related."

"Pickett, bring the first three boxes for case file 10-40-60." He opened up the boxes and took out the first piece.

"We still have to confirm everything, so we are going to run a video tape, okay? Some of the evidence will never be confirmed, but I want you to do your best."

Sara and Jen sat quietly as Melissa went through the first crime photos.

\*\*\*

"In murder cases, the bones aren't buried always. Some are cleaned after the DNA is extracted. The bones are then stored," said Matt.

"In a drawer?" asked Sara.

"Wow, a dead bones archive," said Jen.

Melissa opened up one of the drawers.

"You are a curious bird," said Pickett.

"Yes, with DNA evidence at room temperature the DNA lasts only three months, so the room is cooled much the same as it would be in the grave."

"How does that effect the bones, then?" asked Melissa.

"Good question. Just think, we have recovered DNA from a Neanderthal fossil 70,000 years old. In the human body from the ground, we can extract DNA from the human body 10, 50 even 150 years after death," said Matt.

Pickett took a phone call, "I think we can verify Braeston's first name. Just received a report that Braeston's ID was in the house. His first name is Greg," said Pickett. "Right now he's presumed missing as there is also no record of transit out of the country."

"Okay." Melissa loosened her shoulders which were aching from the stress. "Can I sit for a moment? I hope you aren't expecting me to touch all these bones?"

"Sure, I'll get you something to drink. Water all the way round?"

Matt got on his phone to update Frank, "Yes, Melissa has confirmed earlier that it is Braeston. We have now to wait for DNA testing. Yes, sir."

"You mean I might be able to read 70,000 year old fossils?"

"Wow, Melissa, you are an explorer now."

"Yes, I wonder if what I read is DNA?" Melissa touched some bones. "Oh, my." More images. More stories. Melissa had to sit down.

"What do you see? Do you hear anything? What's it smell like?" Sara had a ton of questions, but Melissa went drawer after drawer completely lost in thought.

"Lunch time," Pickett said with glasses of water in hand, and as Matt was still on the phone, "Matt and I have been given permission to take you to your first crime scene. When we form into little team groups, we give ourselves a name, how about the 5 gang. Makes it kinda fun."

Matt was off the phone and listening, "Sounds good."

*** 

At the crime scene, the 5 gang arrived. They passed through a white metal gate to a red brick house. Pickett turned a key in the lock, and in they walked with their little booties on.

Looking over the photos, Pickett started to put things into context. "The body was found in the living room." He pulled out several pictures of the actual scene. "We found this fingernail close to the body."

Melissa touched the fingernail. "It's not hers."

"How can you tell?" asked Matt.

"See my fingernail? It is smaller." Jen and Sara put their fingers close to the nail.

"We agree. This is not the fingernail of a woman."

"We agree also," said Matt.

"It is male."

"Can you read fingernails?"

She touched it again. Melissa felt like she was on a sky-scraper walking a steel girder, and she was losing her balance. "I'm not sure. I know it is not hers at all, but maybe I need a fingernail to compare it to?"

"They are just trying to figure out how far your gift extends, Melissa."

"Yes, and I think we have a solution to that. Melissa is going to see Jeff again."

"What?"

Sara and Jen were looking at another part of the room. "I suppose we have to pull our weight, and ask the question, if she was strangled, and then shot, reading from your notes here, were there any fingerprints taken from other ghost bullets?" Jen asked.

"Yes," said Matt. "I want you to touch Jeff's hand and his nails."

"Yes," said Pickett, "There were a number of prints found, but one in particular seems suspicious. The fingerprint has been melted off."

\*\*\*

Back at police headquarters, Matt and Pickett pulled Jeff out of his cell into interrogation room "B".

"You can't do this, interrogate me," he said haughtily.

"We are just being friendly. No questions, we just want you to have a cup of coffee. Melissa? Can you come in, please? "Offer this gentleman a cup of coffee," grinned Matt.

"You are up to something. You want my fingerprints," Jeff said.

"You can light your cup on fire if you want," said Matt. "We will give you the match."

Melissa brought in the cup of coffee, touching his hand and his nails in a soft caress."

"Oh, yes, my pretty, you will serve nicely. You are so tempting."

"Here is the match to light your cup on fire, and here is the water to put the burning cup out. You know very well we can't process your fingerprints from that cup as it will not stand up at your trial," said Matt placating him. "See ya later."

"What did you want?" he yelled at Matt and Matt left the room. "Melissa?"

"Don't worry, gang, we will get the DNA another way." They stood behind the two-way glass and watched the DNA go up in smoke. The match went out because it could not stay lit.

After leaving the interrogation area, Sara, Jen, and Melissa were in Matt's office.

Melissa took some deep breaths in, and sat on the couch. "He's reliving the events. They are a little mixed up, and that is difficult to read. So many pictures, Jen."

"Can you take snapshots of it, and review one at a time?"

"Can it work like that? I think she needs a notebook," said Sara.

Matt and Pickett walked back in.

"Yes, we were thinking the same thing. Pickett has several notebooks here for you both, and for Melissa as well as some standard issue police pens."

"What about the fingernail?" asked Pickett. He pulled the fingernail from evidence and gave it to Melissa.

"The fingernails are similar, but this one has a different taste to it. It is as if I am falling from a sky-scraper and I want to vomit."

"You can taste it? What does it taste like?" asked Sara.

"Well, really like trace elements of something. It tastes sweet like candy, but it is not candy. I am confused by this."

Matt and Pickett's eyes were wide open. "You can taste it?"

"Is it his?" Pickett asked again.

"I am not sure."

"Let's look at the report from the lab a little closer, Pickett. It says here under toxicology that the fingernail has poison in it."

"What kind of poison?"

"Arsenic."

"But that has no taste," said Pickett.

"Will this hurt Melissa?" asked Sara nervously.

"It is an orange taste like sugar, and I can't sit still."

"Melissa, are you okay? Here drink some water."

"She'll be fine," replied Pickett. "It's a trace amount."

"Are you sure?" asked Jen.

"Just everyone relax. It will be okay," reassured Pickett.

"We are going to have to get Jeff's fingerprints, and he and Mr. Wright's DNA, and Melissa I want you to write as much down as you can in a time line if possible. We will give you an hour, and then send you home. Step into the next office you three where it is quieter," said Matt.

*** 

"Oh, Mr. Hightechyness is here," crowed Pickett.

"Yes, you two, the lab reports are in. Your Jeff prefers a certain type of car, a Civic. Lucky for you it has a built-in GPS system—email alerts, maps, global messaging, and historical trip archives. Thought I would save you the trouble, and provide you with print outs of all his movements on a time line, and a list of phone calls he made synced to the list. I emailed it to your personal computers."

"Oh, Hightechyness, you are the best," said Pickett giving the high five gesture.

"Anything on the fingerprints from the cars?"

"Yes, fingerprints they have them for analysis now."

Hightechy left the office.

"Do we have the sites of all the murders?"

"Yes, the team has posted that to your wall, and here's the copy on your desk."

"Good. Call a team meeting now."

The teams stopped talking and listened to Matt. There were 36 officers in the room and this included Frank listening in.

"Call down to fingerprints and see if they can match that melted fingerprint to the cars. Pronto. Trace the rest of the fingerprints down, and go and interview any potential witnesses."

Two officers said, "We'll volunteer for the possible witness statements."

"Here is a list of locations of the suspect's vehicles that may have been used in the murders. Mark this list against the murder locations, and start tracing the phone numbers on the GPS, I will provide that in your email," said Pickett.

Four officers signed up for that duty.

"I need another team of four to search the archives for all strangulation cases where a bullet was involved, and provide a report on each," said Matt.

"How are we doing on the witness statements already in progress?"

"Still ongoing, sir."

"Add another six to your team and catch me up on what was done. I expect reports, gentleman."

"Everything in writing, please," Pickett echoed.

"The rest of you answer phones from the public. Every detail counts."

*** 

Matt and Pickett were joined at the hip and turned and went into the office next door with Frank following as well.

"Sara, how is Melissa doing?"

"She's writing like mad and drawing some pictures too."

"Frank, we are working the cases from all angles, but are being held back by forensics. Can you help speed that up?"

"Yes, I will get right on that. I have another team working on notifying the victims' families, and as you know I like to make follow-up calls to that. Anything else you need?"

"Yes, a vacation for a honeymoon?" He looked at Sara and smiled."

"I will arrange for one. For Pickett also?"

Pickett laughed. "I will bring my own date, sir."

"Sara, will you have dinner with me this evening, say 5?"

"Sure. Jen and Melissa are having dinner together with her family."

"Can we go home now?" asked Jen.

"Give Melissa another hour, and then get her mind off things."

"Okay."

\*\*\*

Matt picked up Sara and they sped towards the Beacon.

"We won't talk shop tonight, okay? Just you and me."

Sara smiled and held his hand.

The beacon was full of people. The waitress led them both to a reserved table with a bay window looking out over the water. The pier was in sight.

He sat her down in a chair, but then pulled a jewelry box out of his right pocket. He took her hand and gently kissed it.

"What is this?" she cooed.

She opened it up. "Wow, it is beautiful, a dolphin surrounding a diamond."

"It is just a promise that I love you, Sara. I know it is early in our relationship, too early to ask you to marry me, but I hope now you will consider that I am serious about a proposal."

"Oh yes, I will. Can you help me put it on? How did you know the size?"

"I borrowed a ring from your house as it was part evidence, and I have had a jewelry expert take the ring size for me. I hope you don't mind?"

She held the ring up on her hand and the diamond sparkled. "Wow, you did that for me?"

"I hope you approve?"

"Yes," and she kissed him.

"That was easy. After we order dinner why don't we go out on the pier?"

"Fish, please."

"Me too." Matt scurried off to the kitchen to place the order, and came back with a bouquet of roses. He let her put them in a vase on the table, reached for her hand then led her out onto the pier.

They kissed and held each other tight as the lemon light of the sun caressed them. Slowly, the light was going down and he whispered in her ear, "I am hungry for only you. I love you, Sara."

She kissed him, looking down at the ring Matt had given, and said, "I promise."

***

The following morning, Matt and Pickett arrived early—6 am for a team meeting. Some of the officers had worked 24/7 and now were off shift; others were drinking their first java. With murders to solve, including those at the mound, there were going to be plenty of sleepless nights.

"What do we have?" asked Matt.

"All forensics are done in four cases. Witness statements from all four. Phone records are here for each of those victims," said the Duty Sergeant.

"Worthy of note?"

"Two additional witnesses claim to have seen the killer."

"Really," Matt raised an eyebrow. Matt marched into his office with two of the witness statements. Pickett was tailing him along with the Duty Sergeant.

"Time to read the reports, Pickett."

Matt did a quick scan over the statements. These look good for a possible ID. Get them in to the sketch artists, pronto."

The Duty Sergeant moved quickly to do what was ordered.

"How many DNA hairs did we get?"

"Nose hairs, too, sir?" asked Pickett.

"How many hairs?"

"Several are male. Run the lot through our computer files, and let's hope we get a hit on some of these people."

With that Pickett was off to speak to the Duty Sergeant about assignments. He came back with the fact that he had enough officers, but not enough computers.

"What about the GPS and the victims time lines? Report?"

Pickett handed it to him. Five of the cars have been processed for fingerprints, etc. "Something odd about the prints. The fingertips are melted off too."

"We have our guy," Pickett.

"Officers have tied five of Jeff's cars so far to traffic footage in the area of four victims. More computer power is necessary."

"Pickett, keep reading. I am going to see Frank about logistics." Matt looked at his watch, "What time are Sara, Jen, and Melissa here?"

"10 minutes."

"I'll get us all coffee on my way back."

***

Sara, Jen and Melissa were in the ladies' room at the police station looking over Melissa's shoulder reading her detailed accounts.

"There is a lot there," said Sara.

"You remembered all that?" Jen chimed in with a smile.

"I am doing a section on each person, and it isn't quite finished."

They left the bathroom and met Matt & Pickett in their office. Matt had more files on his desk. In the files were pictures of the victims from family and friends (no reason to show the murder scenes until they had to walk the scenes again). What he wanted was information.

"Can you do this thing with hairs, Melissa?"

"Look, I don't know. Maybe for some of these, but I do know there is another involved in some of this."

"Another?"

"Yes, there maybe two, and they are related, I think. It is hard for me to tell them apart."

"What else?"

"There are more of them," said Sara.

"More women," said Jen.

"Let me look at the pictures you have in the files."

Pickett took the files off the desk and one at a time opened them.

"Yes, there I recognize four and can point out what relates in the notes. The fifth one, I don't know that one at all.

"There are seven more profiles including hairs from the dead files you have to compare with what you already know, Melissa."

"Yes, I can see their faces."

"We will get you in to see the sketch artist right away. We need to see what you have been seeing, Melissa."

Matt, Pickett, Melissa worked through the night, but perhaps a nap on the couch first?" said Sara.

"Right," said Jen backing her up.

"Get the Sergeant in here. Get this journal typed up with the case numbers on the ones that have been identified."

"Please," stated Pickett. We need to confirm any other fingerprints that may be family other than the vics."

***

Jeff's lawyer showed up, and Jeff had to be released. The evidence was in process, but it was building slowly, and Matt and Pickett knew it.

---

"We still have the tracer on the car, and the same officers are on board. They will continue to follow on your instructions, Matt."

"The lawyer isn't going to like that."

"We would have had him for the gun, but that went into the drink."

"How convenient! Did he have any bullets in his pocket?"

"Yes, but they had serial numbers on them. He knew we were coming for him."

"Then we don't have much evidence to go on. Release him."

"Did we get his DNA?"

"No, lawyer did not budge on that."

"Have forensics called. Have them go over the jail cell he was in. When was it last cleaned?"

"In the morning, prior to his being behind bars."

From the window, Matt and Pickett can see Jeff being walked to his stolen car.

"Have the officers pick him up. Now!"

In front of his lawyer, Jeff said, "What now?"

"Put your hands behind your back."

"You son of a bitch!" He looked at Matt through the window.

"What is he being charged with?" ask the lawyer. "This man has rights."

"After Jeff has cleared processing, put him in a line up. Are the two witnesses still here?"

"Yes."

"Have the Duty Sergeant get them prepped for a line up situation right after they complete the artist sketches. And Pickett, you conduct the lineups, and get the lawyer our favorite blend on in house coffee."

Pickett laughed, "Yes, sir. Right on it! Melissa is here."

"Get her in to see the lineup. We are going to have to build several different charges, and hold him separately on each, Pickett."

With that Pickett was off with the lawyer to walk Jeff through processing.

"Duty Sergeant?"

"Yes."

"Get Darren, the car thief, in here. He's in witness protection."

Later, Pickett stood behind glass with the first witness. The lawyer had his coffee and had calmed down, and Jeff arrived in a police lineup.

"Chose carefully," he told the witness. "You must be absolutely sure, Ms. Gavel."

She looked down the lineup, and her eyes fixed on one man. "It's him." She was panicking. "He can see me. He's looking right at me."

"No, he can't see you. Are you sure?"

"Yes, absolutely sure."

"Thank you. This officer here will escort you out and take your statement."

"Yes, it is number 2."

Next, Melissa was called in for the lineup. The lawyer insisted on telling her himself that a man's life was at stake here.

"Yes," confirmed Melissa. "I identify number 2."

"Melissa write everything in the statement. Go with this officer."

The third witness did not give a clear statement. She said number 2 was similar to the man she saw, but different.

Matt came in.

"We have things in process here."

"Add Darren too as a potential witness."

"Yes, Darren was here; he also identified number 2."

Then Pickett showed the lawyer the door and asked him to sit outside.

"Yes, he fired the gun off within city limits. We will add that to the charges."

***

Matt and Picket sat in the office dissecting evidence. Sara, Jen, and Melissa joined them.

"The pictures of the four scenes are telling–birthday parties, anniversaries, weddings," said Pickett.

"Let's read the names out to remember them," said Matt.

"Terry Dent–mid-30's, hair from parent's for victim identification.

Edna King–mid-80's, had her purse snatched. Wrong place, wrong time.

Cindy Trench–mid-30's, lady that left with Jeff at the Edge Bar.

Anita Cummings–mid-30's, found outside the police station in a stolen car."

Sara gently petted Perry, the police dog. "I want to cry." Matt held her hand.

"Me too," said Jen.

"A moment of silence, please," replied Pickett.

What about the hairs next to the bodies?"

Pickett read over the reports. We have DNA on all but two in each case."

"That's odd."

"Seems the unidentified hairs were at all four crime scenes."

Sara said, "So they could be linked, Jen."

"It seems there is not much you can do to identify the hair and the nails, Melissa," said Matt, "But I want you to try again. Anything would help. Besides Jeff likes you," said Matt.

Melissa replied nervously, "Sure...?"

"Try to get him talking about himself."

"I noticed that when he touched me the last time, he was shaving himself in the picture."

Down in the holding cell, Jeff looked sly when Melissa approached with coffee in hand.

"Oh, my pretty is back."

"You must have had a shave recently."

"Oh, yes a few days ago. I normally shave it all off, but they won't let me have the razor. Ha, ha! Would you like to touch my hairy head?"

"Sure? Nice and shiny. Small hairs though. "Here's your coffee."

He sips it. "No good blend. No wonder why the cops are brain dead."

Melissa laughed. She was really getting the hang of using this gift.

"How is your family? Do you have any?"

"Yes, a brother but he's not here anymore. He's dead, okay?"

"Oh, what happened?" She put her hand on Jeff's.

Jeff clammed up, but there were no tears.

"Sorry to hear that." Melissa could see him with paper and water. What he was doing was unclear. He put something into orange juice, and gave it to his brother. She could also see him being buried in the ground.

"He was of no use anyways. I am glad he's gone. No love lost there. All it took was some daily orange juice, and he had a religious experience. He coughed and vomited a lot."

"You gave him orange juice with something in it?"

"Ken was a weakling and didn't like my women, especially my Cindy. I watched him die."

"Yes, pretty. You are different. You will be my best."

"I have to go now," shuddered Melissa.

"We have that all on tape, Pickett. I am going to see Frank, and you can call in his damn lawyer."

"Find this Ken," said Pickett to the Duty Sergeant. "We may have a lead on the case."

"Found him. He's in the computer. Sending a car out to his place."

***

Melissa had figured out where the coffee pot was and brought coffee to the others in the office.

"Did forensics get anything from the pillow in Jeff's cell?"

"They vacuumed the pillow, but sure. Put a rush on it."

Because Melissa had touched Matt when giving him his coffee she added, "No extra charge for telling Sara your feelings."

Matt and Pickett laughed. Then everyone was laughing, but Matt laughed the loudest.

"So, to change the subject, you must know my intentions towards Sara then."

"Yes, Matt. Sara, he really loves you."

Pickett piped up with, "I'm single. Any takers?"

"Melissa touched Pickett's arm, "Oh, you have a very sexy mind. Yes, I will give dating you a try."

Everyone laughed again.

"Well, Pickett, ask for a date," said Sara. "You can come to a dinner at the Beacon. Jen, get a babysitter and bring your man."

"Pickett, the DNA does match the victim, Cindy Trench. We have to get those others identified including the fingernail."

"Any luck on Ken what's his name, the brother?"

"Duty Sergeant, The brother? Have we found him?"

"Yes, Pickett. You aren't going to like this. He was one of the victims found at the mound, sir. Here is the driver's license we found." He gave it to Matt in a baggie.

"Not good, but good. I mean no one wants anyone dead," said Matt.

"Who owns the DNA to a dead body?" asked Jen curiously.

"An autopsy is performed and that is collected as evidence, Jen."

"We have a body in the morgue, so we can ask for a warrant to search the house, including forensics."

"On it," said the Duty Sergeant.

"Maybe the earlier fingernail with match up with Ken?" thought Pickett out loud.

"We need to figure out what Jeff knows about the mound. Go through his records and figure out how Jeff was able to get arsenic from some source."

"On it," said the Duty Sergeant and he flew out of there.

Jen, the Googler, got on the Internet and found an article on different ways to obtain arsenic. Sara and Melissa were reading over her shoulder. "121 poisons offered…freely available on line...fly paper contains 200 to 400 milligrams of arsenic...extracted by putting the paper in water."–The Saint Guardian.com.

Before the day was out Pickett got the list of everything Jeff had purchased with several items highlighted. According to the coroner, Ken was dead for about 3 days.

"Yes, he could have been involved in the murders," said Matt.

"That's what I saw," said Melissa. "The paper in the water."

***

Matt was in Frank's office counting the diamonds and identifying their value–one million dollars! Frank put them back in the safe, spinning the knob.

"We think he killed his brother," said Matt. "We have receipts that he purchased some fly paper."

"You bought some of the same brand?"

"Yes, and the lab is testing a theory that dropping the fly paper in water draws the arsenic out. They say it could be as much as 400 milligrams of poison."

"Have they tested the body as well?"

"Yes, if the results are accurate, we may have the means."

"What have you charged him with?"

"Shooting a gun in city limits. We are also attempting to charge him with purchasing a stolen car."

"What is happening with Darren?"

"His witness statement is different from what Darren told us."

"Is he here?"

"Yes, he's right outside."

"Bring him in. I will handle this as it is a delicate matter."

Darren was brought into Frank's office. "I have been looking over your file, Darren." There was a silence while Frank carefully went from page to page for five pages total.

Darren fidgeted in his chair.

"Now, Darren, Matt reports to me. He seems to think that you are not telling the truth with regard to your witness statement. Why is that?"

"I need to know Matt's assurances in writing."

"I see. Joan, come in here and take dictation for me. Witness protection is provided to Darren providing he tells the truth on his witness statement. What else would you like it to say?"

"That absolves me from being charged with possession of stolen cars, and that I will be relocated with retraining."

"We can't absolve you of any future crimes you may or may not commit Darren, but we will not charge you this time if you are honest in your statement to us. Are we agreed?"

"Yes."

"Joan, go and type that up, please. It will take a few minutes Darren. Joan has speedy fingers. Now, I want you to write the truth on your statement, and then we will exchange papers, okay?"

Joan came back with the letter for Frank's signature, and Frank signed it in front of Darren who handed him his statement.

Frank read out the words, "I sold as many as 10 cars to Jeff. He was told not to hang onto the cars for very long as they were stolen cars. He gave me $300 for each car."

"Is there anything else?"

"No, except he mentioned the women."

"What did he say?"

"My pretties you needed no more graves."

"If anything else comes to you, come and see me and we together will amend your statement."Add now what you know to your statement, please."

Now that was done. Frank walked Darren over to Matt and Pickett's office. "Prepare the charges for the stolen cars for Jeff."

Pickett asked the Duty Sergeant to bring in the security for Darren.

"We have all the reports here, sir, including the fact that Darren identified Jeff in the police lineup," confirmed Pickett. "Now, you are completely afforded protective custody. Go with these officers until the court date. We will call you then as a witness."

"Witness?"

"Yes, you will be fully protected during and after."

The Duty Sergeant came inside the office once more, and said, "There are six bodies from the mound, four are women, and two are men, Mr. Braeston and Jeff's brother. Coroner reports times of death are from 10 years to 3 days for the victims involved."

"How are our sketch artists making out with this?" asked Matt.

"They have called in a facial reconstruction expert."

"We may need more time. I don't know if all of this is enough for Crown to hold Jeff. Pickett and I will work up the summary of the documents for Crown, pass them past Frank who will take them upstairs."

\*\*\*

Jen, Sara, and Melissa were given permission to walk the crime scene of the mound. On the vacant lot they descended down the stairs past the trees outside. The mound inside was cold with the smell of dirt and something else.

"Hello..." said Sara whose voice was thrown back from dirt and timber. She and the others' flashlights were turned on, but Sara swore she could hear her own heartbeat.

Jen saw a really large spider crawl.

Melissa said, "Creepy."

Matt and Pickett joined them there so quietly the women didn't hear them coming.

"Yes..." said Matt.

The women jumped.

"Where are the bodies?" asked Melissa.

"In the morgue," said Pickett.

"Why are we here then?" asked Jen.

"Because...you need to see where people were buried, but there is something else–dead animals," answered Matt.

Pickett pointed out the larger holes and then the smaller ones here, there, and there. "Yes...we thought we should prepare you for what is to come. You are all going to the morgue today."

"Then we are going...but I don't want to," said Melissa.

"I just hate the smell," said Sara.

"It will be my first time," said Jen.

"Yes...you were the distraction for the mortician." Their voices hit the back wall and rebounded.

"Ghosts," said Melissa.

"Happy thoughts, please...,"said Sara.

"There was a squirrel there, a cat here, and a dog there. How are you with animals, Melissa?" asked Matt.

Horrified with the thought Melissa argued with Matt, "No, I am not doing that!"

"We have to take Melissa back outside," said Jen.

"I honestly don't know...I won't. No....."

She has had enough of breathing in the dead," said Sara.

Jen was holding Melissa's hand and they climbed back out of the dirt walls into the open air. "Breathe in confidence, Melissa, breathe out." There were a lot of deep breaths.

Melissa inhaled and exhaled the trees, the sunlight, the moss, the tall grass. A moment ago she felt like fainting, but now she felt more confident and less doubtful, "I will try."

"All right. We will go and have some lunch and wait an hour. Next stop after that will be the morgue," said Matt.

Melissa continued to breathe and Sara and Jen stayed by her side.

*** 

To get to the morgue, there were no steps to go down, just the turning of one's stomach in an elevator ride to the basement. The coroner was there. In the room was steel, tables of steel, drawers of steel, cold hard steel.

"I am cold in here," said Melissa.

The coroner pulled out Mrs. Braeston's body from the drawer.

"So cold," Melissa shivered.

"Let me give you my sweater," said Jen.

Melissa put the sweater on and held her breath and touched the body. Melissa stumbled away. "She ran from the kitchen, hearing Greg cry out. She went to see what happened. He was lying on the floor and not moving."

"Who else is there?" asked Pickett.

"...he... she saw him. It was Jeff."

"Was he alone?"

"No...his brother was there. They chased her down the hall, but the brother grabbed her and pulled her down. He...strangled her, and then Jeff shot her in the head. They moved the bodies to the mound."

"How do you know that?" asked Matt.

"Before she died, she heard them talking about the mound."

"How much of this can you confirm," Matt asked the coroner.

"I can say that she was strangled and died of a gunshot wound. We have more testing of samples including any possible DNA under her fingernails."

"The MO is right," said Pickett. "We have here the report from the Braeston's home. The neighbor said she saw him in the home with another man coming and going."

"Does Jeff have parents?"

"Oh, yes, I have the address here. They are still alive."

"Seems Frank is going to have to notify the family as to the brother's death, and then we will make a visit."

"Good job, Melissa. We are going to get you out of here for now. Too much in a day. Write down your statement, and we will see about coffee, too."

Sara and Jen locked arms around Melissa and escorted her out. It was hard to get the smell out of their lungs on the elevator ride back up to the office.

"How do you guys do this?" asked Sara. "I am still not breathing yet."

***

"Where is Jeff's lawyer?" queried Matt.

Pickett brought him in. He has been sitting out there for an hour.

"It is about time you arrived!" said Matt.

"Yes, you are holding my client without charges and he has rights—"

"I will stop you there, sir, Jeff has charges to answer to." Matt handed him a typed list.

"Well, this certainly won't hold him."

"Now you have the opportunity to meet your client. See you in court."

Matt and Pickett smiled as the disgruntled lawyer left the room.

"We have work to do, Pickett. Where are you Duty Sergeant?"

The Sergeant came in, and Pickett watched Matt snap off some orders to which Pickett added, "Please."

"Get any video taken from the store where Jeff bought the fly paper.

"Make sure we have his purchase receipt.

"What is the status of the fingerprints on all cases?"

The Sergeant was a bit of a genie outside a bottle. He answered up, "We do have the video of Jeff buying it. The fingerprints are all done with names associated except for Jeff's. We have no comparison. Jeff's papers were found at the Braeston's. His name appears on the outside of an accordion filing box. He wasn't much of an assistant administrator: the papers were everywhere and we literally had to comb the box."

"The box ownership is a bit cloudy still, but we have to prove he was not an owner of the house, and that there are no relatives named Jeff." said Pickett.

"We do have a witness statement from the neighbor that he identified himself as the son. Get all of this paperwork in. Check the details again that she indeed saw him and that her statement and the police lineup reflects that," said Matt.

"We will take the paperwork to Crown. Get the store clerk in here. Get that statement and put Jeff back into the lineup for identification," Matt continued.

"Everything will be done," said Pickett. "Thank-you my genie."

"Oh, we need all the fingerprints you have," said Matt.

"What about the other victims? How will we get this guy in jail and keep him there for keeps. You know the courts," said Pickett.

"Next the Braeston's. We have to put him in that house with his stuff. Fingerprints on the box. He was not invited in there to live, and was there under pretense. The Braeston's didn't have a son, do they? By God, we better have another Jeff turn up in this case.., double check, and triple check."

"I had the Duty Sergeant check Mr. And Mrs. Braeston's credit cards," said Pickett.

"And?"

"It seems there were payments made that were not the normal ones after their deaths. Seems the two had quite the thing going."

"Bring back the genie," said Matt. "Have I used up all my wishes?"

"Yes sir," the Duty Sergeant chuckled.

"Get me the works! Phone records. Who called when. Have some of your officer's visit each of the locations where purchases were made that were not normal. Get me the video, and witness statements. Go back 3 months, and after the Braeston's died."

"Right. Anything else?"

"Call a briefing. And make sure your staff gets lunch. Briefing at 1 pm. We need to find out what was the last call the Braeston's made, and where did Jeff and brother take over."

The genie left.

"Pickett, call Sara and extend a dinner invitation for everyone including yourself."

"Yes, that will be my first date with Melissa," Pickett grinned. "She's a fine woman. I always wanted a woman who could read my mind."

"No problem, Pickett. My manager keeps flowers on tap at the Beacon, so no problem. No problem at all."

\*\*\*

Matt and Pickett were talking in the office where the couch seemed very inviting.

"If the Crown, accepts the charges then we can collect a hair sample, fingerprints and DNA for Jeff. What a relief that will be Pickett."

"Yes and we can have that matched to what we have from the crime scenes."

"We must talk to our legal beagle about the fingerprint sample found at many of the crime scenes. It does not have ridges like a normal sample because of the melted fingers. We suspect they are Jeff's but what if we are wrong?"

"Comparisons for the DNA on file will take another week to process."

"Damn, these cases are difficult. There are so many. How did he do such damage below the radar?"

"If we don't get a recordable offence for jail time, we are hooped."

"We need to slam this case shut, Pickett."

"Melissa has been a big help, so have Sara and Jen. I am not giving up my dinner dates. We are just going to have to work smarter."

"Neither am I. Sara's wonderful. I am going to marry that woman. I am so tired though."

"You know where the couch is, and I'll shut the door. Wake you up in one hour."

It was a good thing that Matt could sleep anywhere. Lights out. Sleep just overcame him in the darkness, but there was the feeling of dead weight...Jeff...he buried even more bodies. Matt found one and started digging. There was another skeleton in there somewhere. He saw a bony finger. He kept digging, but the hole kept filling up with dirt. The woods were dead quiet. He couldn't let Jeff get away with it. He kept digging and it was getting harder and harder to lift the shovel.

"Matt?"

"Pickett, where are you?" Matt rubbed his eyes; he was crying and sweaty.

Pickett turned the lights back on. "Are you okay?"

"Just give me a minute." Matt sat up. "There are more bones out there...need to figure out how to dig them up."

"Coffee?"

"Oh, yes," Matt sighed and breathed very deeply, "Too much weight on our shoulders. It is so frustrating trying to get your man when you know he did it."

"I hear you. One just keeps on digging."

"Yes, but the dirt is all here now, and we have to figure it out."

"Just about time to see Sara and crew."

"How many roses do you have?"

"Some of every color."

"A dozen for each then."

"Yes, and I recommend the chef's special, the salmon, and a walk on the pier."

***

"This is going to be five days from hell," said Matt to Pickett. "I have spoken to the legal beagle and the fingerprint guys about the melted prints. We have been assuming," Matt scratched his nose, "that we can use the prints, once they are matched but it could be tricky. Get the legal beagle. What's his name?" Matt snapped his fingers trying to remember.

"Jack," said Pickett. "I will just holler for him as he's two doors down." Pickett walked down the hall and poked his head into Jack's office. "Got a minute?"

Jack arrived at Matt's desk ready for court in a fancy suit and silk tie. "What's up?"

"We need your legal opinion on these prints," said Matt. He passed over a large photocopy.

"Oh, there are no ridges, some but I don't know. You would have to get a match to the person, and it might be difficult to argue that there was no other person who could fit the prints. Do you have other evidence?"

"Working on getting the DNA and fingerprints from Jeff."

"You know I need enough to convict."

"Yes, but what about these particular prints?"

"How many scenes affected by this?"

"We have over 12 cases including the suspected ones for dead archives," said Pickett.

"Okay then, I will go legal beagle on that," Jack laughed, "There must be something on the law books for this."

"We need to get enough on these prints! The techie called and says he has more on the fly paper, and possibly more on the prints. I'll try to get a rush on that," said Pickett.

"I have a court case this afternoon, and I am looking my best. Send me what you have including your fingerprint guy." Jack left.

"Duty Sergeant?"

"Yes, sir. More on those receipts. Jeff also bought toilet paper, and it was from a big chain supermarket. We have determined with the serial number inside the paper roll that it came from this manufacturer."

"What has that got to do with the fly paper?"

"It was purchased the week before the brother died. We checked the toilet paper at the Jeff's apartment. The toilet paper likely came from the same package left at the Braeston's murder scene. There were fingerprints on the used roll, sir."

"I see you are being really thorough in your analysis, and whose prints are they?"

"The melted out thumb and index finger prints, two sets of them, sir."

"Now that is interesting, Pickett."

"Get me those prints!" said Matt, "and the fingerprint guy. Also send a photo to Jack."

"I don't know how these facts are connected yet," said Pickett.

"After you get the statement from Stanley, ask politely for his fingerprints and DNA to rule him out. Carol's, too."

\*\*\*

Sara, Jen, and Melissa arrived in the office.

"After several days in the morgue, I would like to do something else," said Sara.

"Yes, agreed," said Pickett. "I am going to get some information from some witnesses. Do you want to come? We are off to meet Jeff and Ken's parent's home, but coffee first, I think." Pickett went and got the coffee for everyone.

"In the meantime, what have you learned, Sara?" asked Matt.

"There used to be a house on that property with the mound. The property belonged to Jeff's parents the city says. Funny thing is that the house was not that old when it was torn down. It was only 7 years old."

"You are beginning to sound like a detective," said Pickett. He noted the information in his notebook for follow-up.

"Here are our reports on it," said Jen brightly.

Melissa was very quiet, "Jeff and Ken weren't working alone down in the dirt morgue. They had company. I cannot place the voice because of the echo down there. It could be male or female."

"Okay," said Matt, "Maybe we should prepare a bit for the interview with the parents. I will read your report Melissa, and thank you to all of you."

"Sara and Jen, if you get a chance check out the bedrooms Jeff and Ken slept in. Pickett and Melissa you will take the Mrs., and I will take the Mr. At no time are you to be anywhere else so that I can find you easily. Melissa you will touch the two witnesses when we first come in for condolences."

\*\*\*

In an unmarked car, the radio played, "Lost Your Way Get Back Your Soul," and everyone was silent. On arrival they found the property heavily treed, and they knocked at the front door. Next door to the three stairs up was a plastic pink flamingo in the dirt.

"Mr. and Mrs. Bronson?"

He opened the door.

"Yes?"

"Do come in. Call me Stanley and this is my wife Carol."

Some chairs were offered.

Carol broke down in tears, "When will we get our son's body?"

Pickett answered, "The coroner will notify you as soon as is possible."

"Tell me about Ken," Melissa put her hand on Carol's arm.

"Did he live here for a bit while growing up?" asked Matt.

"Yes, in his teenage years." Carol kept sobbing. "He was the weaker of the two boys. Jeff was the strongest."

"So, they grew up in different places?" Pickett asked.

"Yes," said Stanley, "Why, would it be helpful to know where?"

"We would just like a list as we do an extensive background check."

"What for?" Carol quit sobbing.

"Just procedure, Carol that's all."

"Can we see the boys' rooms?"

"Oh, yes, if it will help," said Stanley. "What do you say to the girls making you some tea or coffee, Carol?"

"I would like that."

"So, when did you last see Jeff or Ken, Stanley?"

"A week, come to think of it two weeks back. They mixed some manure out in the garden, but gee it smells really bad this year."

"Do you happen to have a shovel?"

"I have two."

"We'll get the shovel from my car together. It is brand new and I am itching to try it out," said Matt. "Let's go and check out what is going on in the garden."

"I–don't see why not."

Matt nodded to Pickett and then left the house. Matt moved the shovel around in the garden. He dug deeper until he hit something. He dug even deeper, and he uncovered a yellow sun dress.

Stanley collapsed in a heap on the ground. "No," he wailed with his hands to his face. "Don't tell me that my boys did this."

Matt took a deep breath and hoisted Stanley up from the ground, "We don't know anything yet." Matt radioed Pickett, "We need a forensics team down here as quickly as possible. Keep the girls in the house."

"Got it."

Melissa touched Carol again and from the information she started to piece it together, but just listened and said nothing to Carol. Sara and Jen were in the bedrooms.

"Jeff was mean spirited. We didn't know what to do. He shot animals with a gun his father gave him, and he burned them. Ken was soft, quiet, gentle, but followed Jeff's lead. Jeff was always in trouble at school."

"Was there a specific incident you recall?"

"Yes, he made Ken watch as he buried things. One day I caught him yelling at Ken, 'Look, you dumb ass. Do your job!' We thought if we just kept moving, he would grow out of it. We have moved four times, four homes and he never grew out of it."

"Why do you have this uncanny feeling that Jeff did something to Ken?"

"Jeff, was just pure evil," Carol sobbed and all Melissa could do was hold her.

Sara and Jen came back from the bedrooms. "We need to talk more in a bit," said Jen.

"Did your boys keep journals?"

"Oh, yes, they do. We have never read them. The psychiatrist said they should remain private."

"How many of them?"

"I have lost count. The psychiatrist thought they should write about their feelings."

Sara and Jen checked the bedrooms. "There are a lot of journals here."

"Here, too."

Matt came back into the house with Stanley. "This house has been declared a crime scene. A car will come and get Stanley and Carol and take them down to the station."

\*\*\*

Forensics and fingerprint people were in Jeff's parents' house going over everything. One of the techs called to say they had found fly paper in the basement. "There's a lot of it," he said, "Four packages."

Matt sat with Pickett and the rest of the gang over lunch, "I don't feel good."

"Me, either," said Pickett, "I haven't had orange juice for a while now."

"Me too," said Melissa.

"Seems to be a consensus on that," said Sara.

"Just when I think these cases are going to wrap up somehow," said Pickett.

They were all trying to eat sandwiches and swallow down coffee, and Carol and Stanley were sitting in the waiting room trying to eat a sandwich. Carol seems to be able to eat, no problem, but not Stanley.

"What do you think they know?"

"They aren't saying everything. It is like they are hiding something," said Melissa.

"About those journals?" asked Sara. "Jen, did you pick one up and look in it?"

"Yes, it was coded."

Pickett, get the journals cleared through the Duty Sergeant. Pickett was taking a bite out of his sandwich, but rushed off to tell the Sergeant.

Matt sipped the last of his coffee, and Pickett returned with Stanley in tow: it was time to find out what he would tell them.

*** 

"Stanley, what do you know about the fly paper in your basement?" said Matt.

"What fly paper? What has that got to do with it? All right, now. Jeff and Ken were down there the most. I can't get down the stairs with my bum knee."

"You mean when we check, we will not find that you purchased any?"

"I bought some rat poison many years ago, but never fly paper."

"Is there anything to tell us about Jeff and Ken?"

"No, not at all."

"You are being somewhat evasive, Stanley."

Melissa touched him.

"I don't like your tone."

"Did they ever have women over to the house?"

"Yes, they did."

"When was the last one? A girl in a summer dress....Was it the same dress we dug up with a body attached to it?"

"I–I don't know." He shrugged.

"Are you lying, Stanley?"

"Maybe Jeff...where is Jeff?"

"You can see him after we get your statement. Also, if you are willing your fingerprints and DNA to rule out what happened in the garden."

"This way, sir." Pickett met them at the door. "This way, Stanley. Again I am sorry for your loss."

***

"Melissa, how can you tell that Stanley is not telling the truth?"

"No, I see pictures, but there is a feeling, Jen."

"Then how do you know," asked Sara.

"Pretend not to think of something, Jen."

"Okay."

"Now, let me touch you...okay, there is a stuck picture there. It does not move like normal. It has feelings, but it does not move forward."

"Can you tell what the picture is?" asked Sara.

"Yes, Jen, you are at the beach with a little girl. She's swimming. Her head is down in the water. She's wearing the straps of a yellow bathing suit. There isn't a time stamp on this, just that it was in the past, and you were panicking. The feeling is...FEAR."

"Yes, she's my niece, and that day she almost drowned," said Jen.

"Yes, her head is almost submerged. Stanley's picture is with Jeff and Ken. The house is the same one we were in. Stanley is standing over a woman who isn't moving in a yellow dress. She's on the carpet downstairs in the basement. You think the feeling would be one of empathy, but it's not. It is the feeling...of being proud. The picture is really stuck, and I don't think that Stanley has moved past that moment."

"Wow, and all this is in your report?" asked Jen.

"Yes, I had to explain the scenes like this in detail like a photograph of what I saw, and what I felt."

*** 

Matt and Pickett were comparing the Jeff's family's fingerprints. Noted on the report was the word "strange."

"It says here that the two prints for Jeff and his father have the same abnormal similarities," said Pickett.

"Abnormal?"

"The ridges are melted off."

Matt put his own finger to his nose, and raised an eyebrow. "Similar? How are they similar?"

"Very close to each other. Almost identical! The tech said it was very difficult to tell them apart."

"How is that possible?"

"The tech indicates that the only difference is a tiny cut mark."

"Can this get any easier," said Matt with a sigh of frustration.

"No," laughed Pickett, "He says something else."

"What?"

"It matches some of the prints at the various crime scenes so far."

"Wow," Matt got up from his chair and moved around a bit. "We are going to have to get the father back in here, Pickett. See if Carol has any pictures of the previous houses they lived in. Melissa in her report will pay particular attention to their basement."

"I know. Pass it on to the Duty Sergeant."

\*\*\*

Somehow the media had gotten a whiff of a story that someone named Jeff Bronson was in custody. The press arrived outside the police station. Frank had his hands full.

"We have it here you have Jeff Bronson, the Diamond Bullet Strangler."

"This case may or may not be related. We cannot answer any questions at this time due to the nature of the rights of an accused and a trial."

"Have you caught the Diamond Bullet Strangler?"

"It is under investigation."

"Did he do it?"

"Are women now safe in the city?"

"Did he have help?"

"Two people are charged, one being Mr. Wright. Which one did it?"

"Did they both do it?"

"Vigilance is key. Also, any information on these murders that would be helpful to police is greatly appreciated."

"But—"

"That is all. Keep safe out there."

***

Frank was furious. Such heat will come down from the Mayor's office and the police commissioner. He asked his staff, "How did his name get out there?"

One officer replied, "Remember, that charges go public boss, on the record."

"Tighten the lines up, boys. You've worked many late nights on these cases. I want conviction on your part."

"Yes, sir," replied the officers.

"Has the coroner released his complete findings yet? Get him in to see me. Also take your notes and listen, and do not pass forward information to the public. You ask the questions, okay? I mean nothing is to be released at all. Mum is the word."

***

"Two fingerprints and not just one," said Matt munching on a sandwich in the office.

"Yes, we now have comparisons, and now we know the father was involved. Gosh, how is legal going to handle two almost identical prints? I guess I better tell Jack."

"Yes," said Matt.

***

Several days later, the lab came back with further testing on the fly paper and it was confirmed that it was the right amount of arsenic to kill a person. The ballistic report came down on the hand gun from in the Braeston's home, a ghost gun. They had no guns registered to them.

"The bullet was fired at ballistics to get the right type and match the bullets," said Pickett. "Definitely, a .45 caliber. The bullets had no serial numbers on them."

"Got him. Add another charge. Those guns and bullets are illegal here. He was being smart, yes, maybe not. Fingerprints on the gun? On the bullets?"

"Seems the prints are similar, the techs are still trying to figure that one out."

"Damn! These cases are starting to get to me, Pickett. Can you call down there right now and get the very latest info?" Pickett went down the hall making a call requesting the techs call him. He dropped into the legal office. "Jack, come with me." When he got back to the office, Matt had put the call on speaker phone."

"Fingerprints, here?"

"What is the status of the Braeston case and fingerprint comparison?" asked Matt.

"We have prints matching the father and Jeff on the gun, and one set of prints on the bullets."

"Gosh, from a legal standpoint who pulled the trigger?"

Matt and Pickett sat there mulling that one over.

Jack was the first one to speak, "Get back to me, boys on that one."

***

Sara, Jen and Melissa were in the room next door doing assigned tasks.

Melissa was drawing and writing her report like mad. "This is like brain overload."

"Yes," said Jen, "I am writing my report on the bedrooms."

"So am I, and now we have the journals from the house," said Sara. "The code cracker is here, but he isn't sure. What is interesting are the numbers throughout the text."

"I wonder what they mean? Maybe that is the code?" thought Jen out loud. I am in the first journals and maybe there is a master list of the codes or would that be too easy."

"Yes, let us see?"

\*\*\*

Matt and Pickett came into the room.

"Melissa, we need your help with the coffee again," said Matt holding his empty cup up. "Can you do the coffee thing with Jeff's father?"

"Sure, but these journals, I really need to talk with Jeff too to see if we can crack the codes."

"Okay, we are going to talk about the fly paper and the gun with Stanley."

With a big breath in, "I'm ready, Matt."

\*\*\*

Interrogation Room "B". Stanley is brought in, and Frank and Pickett are standing behind the two-way mirror.

Matt began, "Stanley, in the basement you have some fly paper. You say it isn't yours? It is in your house. And what about the gun?"

Melissa touched him. He flinched. Pictures flew. He was there when the fly paper was purchased; he was there when it was put in the orange juice.

"You must come clean, and not lie. Is your statement correct?"

"Well–I can't tell you." He gave a smile.

"What happened, Stanley, after you bought the fly paper? You were there?" queried Melissa.

"It–It's none of your business."

"Well, it's true then?"

"What's that? You knew it was in the orange juice?"

"You were there when the fly paper was purchased and you were there when it was put in the orange juice."

"Yes, that's true."

"Did you know what was in the juice?"

"Ken was weak. What does it matter? He was going to die anyways."

"Die?"

"Yes, he was dying. We would see to that."

"Who would see to that?"

"Jeff and I."

"So what did you do?"

"You know that we were merciful, and did it for the right reasons."

"You gave him the arsenic in his orange juice?"

"For God's sake, yes. He was dying."

"In what way?"

"Cancer."

Melissa turned to Matt and Matt said, "Ken's medical report showed no trace of cancer."

"Then he lied."

Stanley looked down and mumbled.

"Who lied?" asked Melissa.

"Jeff."

"Now, who owned the gun?"

"What gun? I don't know about that."

"The one with your fingerprints on it."

"Oh, that. That was to put them down, and out of their misery."

"Who, the women that Jeff brought home?

"Too many. Lost count."

"Who shot the gun?"

"It doesn't matter...they're all dead."

"Who shot the gun, Stanley?"

"...yes, mumble. We-I shot the gun."

Pickett will take you to amend your statement.

***

His lawyer was present along with Jack who rotated his legal pen on some foolscap. Jeff was brought in to interrogation room "B".

Pickett took the lead. "Your fingerprints are on the gun, Jeff. Did you help your father load the gun?"

"Why would I tell you?"

"Where's the deal?" asked Jeff's lawyer bluntly.

"They know that I purchased the ghost gun." Jeff whispered in his lawyer's ear.

"I don't know anything about that," said Jeff.

"Deal or no deal?" said the lawyer, disdainfully pointing his finger at Jack.

Jack put his pen down after scribbling a note on the foolscap. "For a minimum, it is 20 years. For you, you will get the minimum for just one charge."

The lawyer and Jeff conferred.

"Okay, so he's only up for the one charge?"

"We only have the one charge at the moment," said Jack.

"I purchased the gun and the bullets; I loaded the gun, BANG, but I didn't pull the trigger."

"You handed the gun to your father?"

Melissa came in with coffee and touched Jeff's arm. "What about the journals?"

"What about them?"

"They are in code," said Pickett.

Melissa saw pictures of the base code, and with her photographic memory was going through the pages in her mind.

"Did you strangle anyone, Jeff?"

"Oh no, sir. I was helping my pretties."

"And why am I a pretty?" said Melissa.

"Because your soul needs to be separated from your body into the open air for God."

"And what would you do to free a pretty?"

"I would wrap any cord around her neck and squeeze the air out."

"Did your brother help you?"

"Oh, no. He was too weak."

Pickett grabbed all the murder pictures and placed them one by one in front of Jeff and his lawyer. "Are these your pretties?"

"No, 'er yes, they are all my pretties. Mine all mine."

"We will need your statement to this, Jeff," said Pickett.

Out of the room Melissa asked, "Are we done, Pickett?"

"The statement will be typed up including any audio and video."

"There is one more thing, Pickett. It is about the journals. I have the code, and basically it is a play by play of the murders, each and every one.

"Matt and I look forward to your report."

\*\*\*

It was early in the morning in the time of a waking dream that Melissa was in her room sleeping.

The images of Jeff played on her mind being that she had been in close contact with a serial killer.

The door opened to her room, and Jeff was standing in the doorway. "I have come for you, my pretty." He went off into the kitchen, and tore the extension cord off the toaster.

Melissa tried her best to wake up, but couldn't.

She was now in a scene at the office where Matt and Pickett were saying that Jeff and his father had escaped.

In her dream, the dog was barking, but she couldn't wake up. She was stiff from fright.

Jeff came to her bed, and said, "Not only can I feel you, but also sense your pulse. Yes, my pretty," and he bent down, pulled her by her hair, and wrapped the cord around her neck. "This daddy, you can't stop me."

Melissa was choking and woke up with a start to a knock at the door. Jen and Sara were there.

"We received a telephone call from Matt and Pickett," said Sara.

"Yes," said Jen hysterically.

"What?" said Melissa gasping, "Out with it."

"Jeff and his father, Stanley, were released on bail."

"No...no, no! He-they can't get out."

"The judge said he was not a flight risk, and let him out," said Sara.

"He—he was just here. He wants to come here," said Melissa."

They sat down on the couch.

"He—he sees his murders in advance. He was choking me."

"How?" asked Jen.

"Yes, both he and his father set up the crime scenes."

"Oh, God!" said Jen.

"We have to get everyone in one room," said Sara. "I'll call Matt." She touched her heart necklace that Matt had given her.

"I will go get my family myself."

"No, we won't split up."

"Call your husband first, Jen."

Jen put her phone on speaker phone. The phone was dropped.

"Jen, he's choking your husband. We must get over there."

"Matt says to leave the line open. They will be here in 5 minutes."

Sara said, "We have to take the dog with us. Hurry...."

"Yes," they heard a man's voice as Jen turned the lock on her door, "Take out the male and the dog first, and then we will have the time, son."

"Jeff! The dog is barking, but where's the father?" asked Jen.

"I am here for you...."

Stanley was standing behind the door with a gun. Jen gave the dog the command to attack, and Melissa gave her dog the command. Two dogs were on the father. Jeff had a cord around her husband's neck, and he lay gasping on the floor. Jen ran at Jeff and with as much force as possible pushed him off, loosening the cord.

The gun went off. Sara's dog screamed in pain. The father dropped the gun.

Jen's husband was on the flour, not breathing. Jen was giving mouth to mouth. Jen called her dog and gave a command to attack Jeff. Jeff was fighting off the dog.

Sara grappled with the father for the gun. It went off again. The shot whizzed by Melissa's forehead.

"Jen, watch out Jeff," squealed Sara.

Jen grabbed a lamp off the table next to the TV and struck him on the head with it. The force shattered the light bulb. Jeff was down on his knees and Jen went for the masking tape that she had from moving some boxes that morning. Together she and Melissa held him down and tied him up. Jen went to her husband to see if he was breathing. He coughed. He was alive....

Sara grabbed the gun and held it on Stanley.

Matt and Pickett arrived. Other officers were there, too, with guns pointed.

"Matt, we need an ambulance for medical attention, including one of the dogs."

Later that day, Jen's husband was given a sedative and kept overnight. And Jen's mom took the little one who had cried through everything.

\*\*\*

Seems not one of the gang could sleep, and they ended up in an all night diner on 16th street called, "Shakey's". They served the most amazing cheesecake with a coffee to wash it down. They drove to the police station where all three gave witness statements.

"They won't get away with it this time," said Matt.

Frank was awakened in the middle of the night to come down to the police station at 3 am. He gathered his men, and barked details for the shift.

"Both men are processed now," replied the Sergeant, "and we have the boys and crew working on paperwork."

Frank nodded.

"We found the rest of the diamonds in the father's pocket."

Frank was given a small velvet bag and looked inside.

"How much?"

"A million dollars give or take a few dollars," said Matt. He walked with Frank to his office.

"That solves the jewelry robbery," said Frank. "The owner will be glad to get back his stolen property."

In came Sara, Jen and Melissa, "It is time for more coffee," said Melissa and they all laughed.

"Seems you three apprehended two suspects and would make excellent officers. The dog that was injured has been treated and will get some time off. Which one was it?

"Max, the security dog, sir," said Pickett.

"What say you to becoming officers and going through the police academy?"

"Become one of us," said Matt.

"And have more coffee," said Pickett.

"We have just had cheesecake, sir," said Jen.

"Can we have some time to think about it?" said Sara.

"I need a vacation," said Melissa.

"All expenses paid by the department," said Frank, "And citations for bravery, for each and every one of you."

On Vancouver Island, there was a double wedding ceremony in progress…. Sara and Matt, Pickett and Melissa were saying their marriage I do's when a shot rang out.

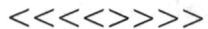

# About the Author

**Wendy Tarasoff, BA**

*Pen Name Wendy Turner*

Wendy realized words and sentences made the difference for her writing. She went from writing E letter grade papers to writing an A++ play.

She grew up in an oral tradition household telling stories around the kitchen table, and worked as a waitress, gas jockey, and then as a secretary. She completed her degree in English at Simon Fraser University whilst eating a lot of chocolate. Wendy won an Award for Poetry: The judges for the poetry competition were Mayor Wright from the City of New Westminster, and one of two Poet Laureates in Canada, Mr. Don Benson.

She has published three children's books—*Scare Away the Dark, Dragon's Pearl,* and *Freddie, the Talking Mouse. Freddie* is in English and Spanish versions. She has also written the *Secret Sauce of Sentences,* a book for you on sentence structure. Wendy has just put the finishing touches on a Romance Murder Thriller, *Diamond. Diamond* is available in both English and Spanish versions.

Her work can be found at Amazon.com under her real or pen name listed at the front of the book after the title page. She also helps fellow writers get their writing edited for Amazon.com. In addition, she has designers on tap for your special book cover.

**Reach Wendy directly at wtarasoff7@gmail.com.** Please leave a review of the book on Amazon. I appreciate your feedback.

www.ingramcontent.com/pod-product-compliance
Lightning Source LLC
Chambersburg PA
CBHW071349170626
46811CB00003B/1053